NEWS AND NUTMEG

A SMALL TOWN COZY MYSERY

CARLY WINTER

Edited by
DIVAS AT WORK EDITING

Cover by
COVEREDBYMELINDA.COM

WESTWARD PUBLISHING / CARLY FALL, LLC

THE TRI-TOWN MURDERS

News and Nectarines

News and Nachos

News and Nutmeg

News and Noodles

NEWS AND NUTMEG

Was it death by donut or something far more sinister?

Drama ensues when the president of the Oak Peak knitting club is found dead, a half-eaten donut at her side.

When the death is ruled a murder, reporter Tilly Bordeaux is tasked with writing the story. As she dives into the life of the deceased, she uncovers a woman who attempted to make a stand for herself, but instead, made enemies with everyone.

As the list of potential killers becomes longer, Tilly's desire to find the murderer grows. When she confronts the killer, a shocking scandal is revealed that will set the Oak Peak gossip vine on fire and give

Tilly the biggest story of her career... if she can survive.

1

———

"YOU'RE the only person I know who has thrown up and fainted during a marriage proposal."

I glared at my friend across the table in her bakery, Debbie's Deliciousness. The scents of nutmeg and cinnamon hung heavy in the air. It had been about six weeks since that debacle, and she brought it up at least every four days. Frankly, she was beginning to irritate me.

"You don't need to remind me," I said. "It wasn't one of my better moments."

My boyfriend, Derek York, had proposed to me at the Halloween dance right after we'd won the best costume contest. Debbie hadn't exaggerated. I'd literally tossed my cookies all over him as he knelt down before me, and then I'd fainted and knocked my head so hard, they'd rushed me to the hospital, fearing I had a concussion.

Glancing out the window, the snow came down in a wet sheet. The little town of Oak Peak did a pretty good job of keeping the main streets plowed during the winter, but I lived out of town and driving the two-lane highway home would become dangerous very soon.

I had to go visit Lydia Tillwacker, the president of the Tri-Town Knitting Club, and I needed to get moving. Why the knitting club had a president, I didn't know, but they seemed to do a lot for the community. Last year they'd done Handsies for the Homeless, and this past October they'd participated in Booties for Babies. Lydia wanted to talk to me about their next project, Cozies for Christmas, and I had no idea what that entailed. I'd learned that the group, and especially their esteemed leader, Lydia, liked to have their names and pictures in the paper. Since important news in our little triangle of the world rarely happened—except for the last two murders—I was happy to have something worthy to write.

"Your place looks really festive, Debbie," I said, turning back to her. In the corner of the bakery sat a six-foot-high Christmas tree with different color decorations and gold and silver lights. The same color of tinsel dangled from the register and the display cabinet. She'd also hired someone to paint a mural of a smiling Santa standing in the snow with two children running toward him on her windows.

"Thank you. With all the money Carla is saving me, I can really get into the spirit."

My friend Carla now worked with Debbie. I never thought the relationship would be a beneficial one, but they got along well with Carla taking care of the business end, Debbie baking, and both greeting customers at the popular bakery.

"Where is she?" I asked.

"Taking a much-needed day off. That woman busts her butt just as hard as I do. I'm so lucky she came aboard."

Usually a total control freak, Debbie had found the perfect pairing in business with Carla, and they had truly formed a great partnership.

"Ugh. I wish this snow would stop," I mused. "Winter has just started and I'm already sick of it."

"Think of it this way: we need the water. We live in this tinderbox called California. And if you complain about the snow again to me before April, I'll put real sugar in your coffee."

I gasped and placed my hand over my heart as if I was truly offended. "You wouldn't dare."

"Test me and find out."

We both burst out laughing. Even though Debbie owned a bakery, she'd been one of my biggest cheerleaders in my slow and steady weight loss. She'd even come out with a line of sugar-free donuts made with wholesome sweeteners and profited nicely. Whether she'd done it for me or noticed the people in the Tri-Town region had grown very 'thick,' as she said, I didn't know because she'd mentioned both.

The bell on the door rang, and we turned to see who had entered. Mrs. Marple stomped in, her gray hair looking a little flat from the moisture in the air, her mouth in a fine, angry line as snow jumped from her boots.

She slipped off her mittens and shoved them into the pockets of her bright purple parka, then hung the coat on the rack by the door, all the while muttering something indecipherable.

"What can I get for you today, Mrs. Marple?" Debbie asked as she stood and hurried behind the counter. "Would you like the usual?"

The older woman walked over as she clenched and released her fists. "This cold weather is doing a number on my arthritis. I'll have a café au lait, Debbie, and I'll take one of those cinnamon and nutmeg donuts."

"Yes, ma'am," Debbie said. "If you'd like to join Tilly and me at the table, pull up a chair. Or, if you prefer to enjoy my delicacies on your own, we won't be offended."

"I'd love the company," she replied. "Thank you."

As I grabbed a chair from the next table, Mrs. Marple walked over, then sat down. "How are you today, Tilly?"

"I'm fine," I replied. "I do wish the snow would go away, though."

"Hey!" Debbie yelled from behind the display case. "I told you, no complaining!"

Mrs. Marple grinned and rolled her eyes. "What fun is winter if you can't grumble about it?"

"Exactly," I agreed. "It's like the heat in summer. It's almost rude not to mention the temperature."

Debbie joined us a moment later with Mrs. Marple's order. When we were all situated, Debbie turned to the older woman. "What are you up to today? You're in a bit early."

"I had to go see Lydia Tillwacker," Mrs. Marple replied with a sigh. "We were discussing our Christmas project for the knitting club."

"What's that going to be?" I asked. "I'm supposed to head over there today to interview her."

"Well, I personally think we should do something for the homeless shelter again, but she wants us to make booties and blankets for the babies in the hospital and call it Cozies for Christmas."

"That's cute," Debbie said with a shrug.

"Yes, it's a cute name, but I think the homeless shelter can use the blankets more than the babies in the hospital. I just want to put our resources and talents to good use and where it's needed, especially during the winter season."

Frankly, I agreed with Mrs. Marple. The hospital had supplies. The homeless shelter always needed things to help people stay warm.

"But anyway, she didn't see my point," the older woman continued, shaking her head. "She can be so pigheaded sometimes and she runs the knitting club with an iron fist."

I'd never seen that side of Lydia before. Each time I'd interviewed her for an article about their projects, she'd been very upbeat and kind.

"What's to run in the knitting club?" Debbie asked, her brow furrowed.

"It began a few of years ago with a group of us ladies who wanted to meet, chitchat, drink a little wine and do something nice for the community. It was a social gathering for us. We didn't need the articles in the Tri-Town Times. Then Lydia got involved. You would think she was running a Fortune-500 corporation with the way she's always talking about how we have to expand our marketing efforts and our output. Our meetings are no longer fun gatherings, and some of the ladies feel as though Lydia has turned the group into a sweatshop. We never produce enough to make her happy, and we're all sick of it."

"That's too bad," I said, mildly surprised at the drama. They were a bunch of old women, and I'd always hoped that as I aged, people would become more flexible and pleasant. "Maybe some of you who don't like what she's done should break off and go back to the way things were."

Mrs. Marple nodded. "Believe me, it's been discussed, and I was the one nominated to bring up our dissatisfaction to Lydia. It was another reason I went there today. She wasn't pleased with me at all."

"What did she do?" Debbie asked, her eyes gleaming with curiosity. I could see she would be filing away the conversation to discuss in the future.

"Oh, her behavior was awful," Mrs. Marple said, glancing around the bakery. "I don't like to gossip."

"You're among friends," Debbie said gently. "And it sounds like you need to vent a little. If you want to tell us what happened this morning, we're here to listen."

Mrs. Marple grinned and took a sip of her coffee while casting her blue gaze on my friend. "You aren't going to get me with that line of nonsense, Debbie."

I bit my lip to keep from laughing. Debbie loved gossip, and Mrs. Marple knew it.

"Okay, well then, dish the dirt!" Debbie said, throwing her hands up in the air. "Don't leave me hanging, lady!"

The three of us all burst out in giggles, and Mrs. Marple shook her head and she wiped her eyes. "I'm so glad I stopped in today. Lydia really got under my skin. I was furious when I walked in, but I feel much better."

Debbie and I stared at her expectantly.

"When Lydia named herself the president of the knitting club, she had each of us sign a contract stating we would remain a member for a minimum of one year. At first, we all thought it was silliness... I mean, it's a social occasion for those of us who enjoy the craft. We all signed while snickering behind her back. Little did we know she has a bit of Stalin and Hitler buried underneath that sweet façade."

"She didn't like when she heard the troops wanted to leave the field, huh?" Debbie asked.

"Not one bit. I told her today it wasn't any big deal and she needed to consider her blood pressure. She screamed all sorts of profanities at me before I left, and even waggled the contract I'd signed in my face. Then she had the audacity to tell me she'd take me to court if I left the group and others followed."

"For what?" I asked. "It's a knitting club!"

"Not to Lydia," Mrs. Marple replied. "She said she'd sue me for breaking a contract and contractual desertion. I wanted to beat her over the head and knock some sense into her."

I furrowed my brow, unable to believe that this silliness came from the knitting club. "Is that even a thing? Contractual desertion?"

"Beats me, Tilly. However, my ancestors founded this town, and no one is going to speak to me the way she did. I believe I deserve, and have earned, a little more respect than she showed me." Mrs. Marple sniffed and took another sip of her coffee. "We're supposed to have a meeting tonight, but I refuse to attend. When I get home, I'm calling the others and telling them about my interaction with Lydia, and her threats. This won't go over well with any of them."

As Mrs. Marple stood, Debbie and I followed her to the door and helped her with her coat.

"Goodbye, girls," she said as she grabbed her purse and gave us a wink. "Be good, but not too good."

"You stay out of trouble, Mrs. Marple!" Debbie called as we watched her shuffle through the snow to her car.

"I can't believe that," Debbie murmured. "What a bunch of crazy old bats."

"All that drama over knitting," I said, retreating back into the store. "I've got to go see Lydia today. I hope she's not mean to me like she was to Mrs. Marple."

"Did you sign a contract with her?"

"Of course not."

"Then I think you'll be fine. She was in yesterday afternoon picking up a box of donuts for the meeting tonight and was as sweet as the snow is white."

I slipped on my coat. "She may very well have a lot of leftovers."

"She might not even have a meeting at all. It sounds like the knitting club is declaring mutiny and she'll have a dozen donuts all to herself."

Debbie and I hugged, and then I pulled my keys

from my parka. "I'll talk to you later," I said. "I'm heading out to see Queen Lydia right now. It should be interesting to hear what she has to say about the Christmas project. She may be the only one working on it."

"You'll have to call me when you leave her," Debbie said. "Let me know what happens."

"Yes, ma'am. And just for the record, I hate snow."

I shut the door behind me before Debbie could chastise me for complaining.

Would I meet the sweet Lydia Tillwacker I had become used to, or the tyrant Mrs. Marple had described?

2

———

THANKFULLY, Mrs. Tillwacker lived close to Oak Peak Avenue, the main drag of town where I worked. As I slowly rolled through the snow toward her house, I thanked the heavens for my four-wheel drive. It definitely seemed that my trip home would be long and grueling.

I pulled my pickup over to the curb and sighed in relief while setting the gearshift in park, took my keys, and slipped out of the cab into the cold. After wrapping my scarf around my neck, I stuffed my hands into my parka and headed up the pathway to the front door. The steps to the home looked a little slick, but the footprints in the snow indicated someone had already trudged up and down them. Probably Mrs. Marple.

A sheet of ice had formed under the snow, and I went down on the third step. I cartwheeled my arms as I flew backward through the air and landed on the cement walkway. Staring at the gray sky for a moment while the snow fell, I tried to catch my breath and evaluated if I'd broken anything. Somehow, I'd avoided hitting my head. The last thing I needed was another trip to the hospital.

I slowly sat up, then staggered to my feet while eyeing the stairs. This time, I'd hold on to the railing. When I made it to the porch, I brushed off the snow and stomped my boots, hating every single fleck of the white stuff. Although, the Tillwackers' side yard reminded me of a winter wonderland with the pristine white powder covering it, and it was really pretty. I admired the tranquility for a few brief moments.

After knocking on the door, I waited patiently for a couple of minutes, then tapped again. I bended and flexed my arm and realized my shoulder must have taken the brunt of my fall when pain radiated from there.

Glancing behind me, I wondered if I should just leave. Lydia had told me to be at her house at eleven, and here I was. Where had she gone? Mrs. Marple had left there not too long ago.

My annoyance at my fall grew, as did Lydia's absence. I pounded on the door again, this time with a little more force. Perhaps she had a hearing problem I wasn't aware of. "Mrs. Tillwacker?" I yelled. "Are you home?"

Minutes went by without an answer, so I tried the knob. To my utter shock, the door opened and my frustration turned to gut-churning worry. I stared at the panel for a moment, then took a step in. "Mrs. Tillwacker?"

Memories of finding Mr. York, my neighbor, gasping for life in the tall grass outside his home haunted me. Except at this home, there wasn't anywhere outside for Mrs. Tillwacker to be. She resided in a tidy neighborhood with small lots, while Mr. York and I both had large plots of land.

I called for her again as I slowly made my way into the kitchen. Perhaps she had fallen and needed my help? I wouldn't hesitate to find her like I'd done with Mr. York. Worrying about whether I'd discover him naked or in some other odd situation and what our relationship would be like afterward had held me back from searching for him. Maybe if I had discovered him a few moments earlier, I could have called the ambulance sooner and he'd be alive today.

No, I'd search for Lydia and apologize later if I found her in bed or in the bathroom.

In the empty kitchen I found the box of donuts from Debbie's Deliciousness open and one missing. I headed up the stairs, the navy-blue carpet muffling my footsteps. No one in the first bedroom. Done in browns and with minimal furniture, I could tell it was a guest room. The second room was definitely lived in—clothes strewn on the floor, pictures of a young woman with friends hanging from the dresser mirror and the unmade bed all a dead giveaway.

But it wasn't Lydia's room. In her sixties, there was no way her bottom would fit in the thong I tripped over.

The room at the end of the hallway would be considered the master. More spacious, it contained a king-sized bed neatly made with a yellow comforter. The faint smell of Ben Gay hung in the air.

"Mrs. Tillwacker?" I yelled again. When no one answered, I hurried down the hallway and stairs back to the first floor.

Nothing in the dining room.

The living room was where I discovered her.

She lay in the middle of the floor face up, her eyes staring blankly at the ceiling, a half-eaten donut at her side. The fireplace raged and made this room warmer than the rest of the house.

I hurried over and felt her wrist for a pulse while I pulled out my phone and dialed 9-1-1. After giving the operator the address, I sat in the chair farthest away from Lydia.

Her skin had been warm, but there hadn't been a pulse.

Placing my elbows on my knees, I cradled my head in my hands as tears welled in my eyes. I didn't want to look at her.

How and why did this keep happening to me?

The crackling of the fire was the only thing that interrupted the silence in the room. Moments later, I heard the sirens, and I stood and went to the front door.

The ambulance pulled up behind my truck and the two EMTs, both male, rushed in. "Where is she?"

I pointed to the living room and followed them in at a distance, then stood in the doorway as they examined her.

"She's dead," the one on the left said. "Looks like she choked on a donut."

"Are you related?" the second guy asked.

"No," I said, shaking my head. "We had an

appointment at eleven. She was like this when I arrived."

"This is probably an accident, but the cops should be here soon."

On cue, sirens once again wailed in the distance. It would be my luck and right on track with my day if Sheriff Connor would be the one to catch the call.

To my dismay, he'd been reelected a month ago in a landslide. I'd wanted to investigate if there had been election fraud, but my boss, Harold, had put the kibosh on that. Instead, he encouraged me to attempt to have some type of positive relationship with the man I found to be a condescending, misogynist pig. It would be good for the paper to have a cop who shared information with us, but I just couldn't bring myself to kiss his butt.

I glanced over at the front door and groaned as our gazes met.

"Why are you here?" he asked.

"She found the body," the paramedic answered.

"You've got to be kidding me. Tilly, is that true?"

"Yes," I said with a sigh. "It's true."

The sheriff chuckled and placed his hands on his hips. "Unbelievable. You're like a hatchet man... or a black widow. I'm glad I'm not married to you."

"Like that would ever happen," I muttered.

"Excuse me?"

"Nothing. I'll wait in the foyer until you're ready to take my statement. I know the drill."

He nodded as I turned and walked to the front door. If it hadn't been so darn cold, I would have waited outside, but the last thing I needed was to get myself a case of frostbite. Instead, I stared out the skinny window to the left of the door. I should have just minded my own darn business instead of swooping in like I wore a cape. Hindsight was always twenty-twenty.

As Deputy Byron Mills rolled up in his cruiser, I came to the conclusion the day couldn't get any worse. We'd dated briefly after my divorce. I'd found him nice to look at but he bored me to tears. Unfortunately, he still had feelings for me. I took a few steps back so he wouldn't swing the panel into my face. My shoulder already hurt. I didn't need a black eye as well.

His gaze widened when he saw me. "What are you doing here?"

"I had an appointment with Lydia Tillwacker today at eleven. I was the one—~

"Wait! Don't tell me. You found the body."

"Yes."

"Wow, Tilly. Did you know that in my years of

policework, I've never been the one to discover the dead? And here you are, on number three in a year. How does that happen?"

"I wish I knew," I said. "I was going to leave when she didn't answer the door, but then I wondered if she was in trouble and maybe I could help her."

"How did you get in?"

"I opened the door. It wasn't locked."

Byron rolled his eyes. "Okay. We'll see about that." We stared at each other for a moment, and then his features softened. "How are you, Tilly?"

"I'm... I'm fine."

"How's Derek?"

"He's fine, thanks for asking."

"I heard about what happened at the Halloween dance."

"Pretty sure everyone has," I said, staring at the floor. There had been hundreds of people at the party and they'd all gone home and told the story. I still heard people whispering about me while out and about.

"A marriage proposal should be a happy thing," Byron continued. "Not make you throw up all over your suitor. That may be something for you to consider in your future plans."

Of course it should have been a happy occasion,

and I'd had enough of hearing about it. "Thanks for the advice, Byron. It's appreciated."

I stomped out of the house and decided to wait on the porch. The chance of freezing to death was better than staying in the same room with him and his boss.

A half hour later, my teeth were chattering and my body trembled when Byron stepped out.

"You okay, Tilly?"

"Y-yes."

"They're going to bring the body out. After that, why don't you come inside and I'll get your statement from you really quick?"

"Okay."

"Why didn't you just wait in your car if you didn't want to be in the house?"

I stared at my truck, and I had no answer for him. Apparently, I had become too upset for rational thinking.

The medics rolled the gurney past me and down the stairs. I noted that they didn't even slip. Then, I stepped into the foyer with Byron.

"Let's get your statement right here," he said. "The sheriff is still doing his investigation in the living room."

"Fine."

I blew into my hands as he took out his notebook.

"So you had an appointment with her at eleven?"

"Yes. We were going to discuss the knitting club's Christmas project so I could write a piece on it for the paper."

"And what happened when you got here?"

"I knocked on the door and when no one answered, I pounded on it pretty hard. I probably got a little frustrated and tried the door. When it opened, I thought maybe she was in trouble, so I went in and searched the house. I found her, then called 9-1-1."

"Did you touch anything? Move anything?"

"I may have grabbed the banister on my way to the second floor, and I definitely used the one outside. The only thing I touched was her neck when I looked for a pulse."

"Okay, good," Byron said, and snapped his notebook shut. "She probably choked on a donut, or maybe tripped and hit the back of her head on the table or something like that. The sheriff doesn't see any signs of foul play, but we'll leave that call up to Doc Wheeler."

The town doctor doubled as the coroner when needed and had a remarkable resemblance to Tony

Stark, or Ironman, and was also friends with my boss, Harold. We'd probably know what happened to Mrs. Tillwacker before the police, or shortly after.

"Do you want me to call you when we find out?" Byron asked.

His demeanor startled me. We hadn't been on very pleasant terms. He didn't like Derek and certainly didn't like me dating him. I had pleaded that we remain friends, but he'd still been snappy and rude. Now he wanted to phone me when Mrs. Tillwacker's cause of death had been discovered?

Interesting.

"Sure," I said. "That would be nice. Thank you."

He reached out and grabbed my hand, then gave it a gentle squeeze. As our gazes met, I noted the feelings he still had for me. I couldn't hold his stare, and I gently removed my palm from his grasp.

Without another word, I turned and headed out the door, determined to drive straight home and put this awful day behind me.

Hopefully, Mrs. Tillwacker had died from choking on her donut, and not something far more sinister.

3
___

I followed a plow home. It took over an hour, but at least I didn't have to concentrate too hard on the slippery roads.

When I pulled into my driveaway, Derek stepped out onto the porch with Tinker and all my worry seemed to fade. Tinker didn't bound through the snow to meet me, which meant she'd probably been holding her urine for most the day. My Golden preferred dry, sunny days, not cold and wet ones.

As I trudged through the snow, I kept my gaze downward and carefully studied where I put my feet with each step. One fall for the week was enough.

"Hey," Derek said as I ascended the stairs. "How was your day?"

I wrapped my arms around his neck and sighed as he pulled me close. "Awful."

"Oh, no. Come inside and tell me about it."

We walked arm in arm through the door and into my cozy home. Something cooked in the oven, and the smell of garlic and ginger wafted through the house, making my mouth water. The fireplace crackled in the living room while Derek helped me slip out of my coat and take off my boots.

Since the debacle at the Halloween dance, not much had changed between us. We did spend most of our time at my home since I had all the animals that needed to be fed, but we weren't engaged. We'd decided to hold off on that idea for a bit and Derek admitted he'd gotten carried away by asking me so soon since we hadn't even known each other for six months.

However, my feelings for him only continued to grow daily. What girl wouldn't like a guy who stuck around after being vomited upon?

"I made some hot chocolate," Derek said. "Go sit by the fire and I'll bring it to you."

He wouldn't get any arguments from me. I plopped down on the couch and Belle came off the windowsill to greet me by sitting in my lap and immediately continuing her snooze. Tinker curled up at my feet.

"You need to go out at some point," I said to the dog. "You can't hold it forever."

She glanced up at me with big brown eyes and I could have sworn she'd understood every word I'd said. I also got the feeling she was going to ignore me.

"Here, Tilly," Derek said, handing me a mug then sitting down next to me. "What happened?"

"Well, I had an appointment with Mrs. Tillwacker today to learn about the knitting club's Christmas project."

"Yes. I remember you telling me about it."

"When I got there, she didn't answer the door." I took a sip of my hot chocolate and found it to be the perfect temperature. Not scalding so it burned my lips, but warm enough to take the chill off. "I almost left, but then I knocked really hard and became frustrated that she was standing me up, so I tried the handle. It opened."

"Uh-oh."

"Yes. To make a long story short, I found her dead in the living room."

He draped his arm around my shoulder, coming dangerously close to my bruise from the tumble down the stairs. "I'm assuming you called the police?"

"I did."

"What did they say?"

"Byron told me that Sheriff Connor thinks she either choked on a donut or she tripped and hit her head on the table or something."

"So he doesn't think she was killed?"

I shook my head.

"Well, I'm sorry you had to go through that today. I'm glad you're home safe and sound."

With that, he gave my shoulder a squeeze and I leapt from the sofa. Hot chocolate swished out of my cup and onto Tinker.

She didn't seem to mind as she gave it a sniff and began to lick it.

"What was that about?" Derek stared at me wide-eyed. "What happened?"

After I set down my mug, the tears started and exhaustion overtook me. "I fell down the stairs and hit my shoulder. I hate the snow."

"Oh, Tilly. Come here."

I moved back over to the couch and collapsed into his embrace.

Why he stuck around, I didn't understand. Who

wanted an accident-prone woman with the panache of finding dead people?

As I cried on his shoulder, I realized that Derek did. He'd seen me at my best, and my worst, and he never went anywhere. We'd met with me threatening to beat him with a baseball bat, and even after that rocky start, he hadn't shied away.

He had become a very important part in my life, his stability a godsend.

When my tears had run dry, I curled up at his side.

"Do you want to watch some television?" he asked.

I nodded, and he grabbed the remote.

It wasn't long before I fell fast asleep.

THE NEXT MORNING, we woke to sunny skies and I felt much better. My "life sucks" attitude had disappeared, and I was ready to take on my day. I made sure Tinker did her business outside before I kissed Derek goodbye and left.

With the streets only being wet and not icy, my ride to work went by smoothly. After parking in front of the Tri-Town Times, I walked in to find Doc

Wheeler talking to Harold. Both stood and smiled while greeting me.

"How are you today, Tilly?" Doctor Wheeler asked. "I understand yesterday wasn't the best for you."

"No, it wasn't," I said as I set my bag down on my desk. "I'm feeling much better today, thank you for your concern."

"Excellent." Harold rubbed his palms together. "Looks like we've got ourselves another murder."

My heart sank. "Seriously? Who?"

"Unfortunately, I believe that Lydia Tillwacker was killed," Doctor Wheeler said. "She didn't choke on a donut as the sheriff insinuated. I think she was struck from behind with a long, thin object."

"What about her tripping and hitting her head on a table or something like that?"

I really wanted Lydia's death to be an accident, not another murder.

"Well, I've looked at the room and I didn't locate a table that matches the injury I found."

"But there wasn't any blood!"

"You can sustain head trauma and die without a drop of blood being spilled, Tilly," Doctor Wheeler said softly. "I'm afraid she was hit from behind. I'm thinking perhaps something from the fireplace set was used as the weapon."

I sat down behind my desk and recalled the tidy, metal tools sitting next to the roaring flames—a brush, log lifter, shovel and poker.

"It's the only thing in that room that makes any sense," Doctor Wheeler continued. "Of course, the perpetrator could have brought in the weapon, but right now, I think that's the best bet. I'm going to have the set tested for DNA. There are a lot of fingerprints on them, but I would expect that with the fireplace being used during winter."

"Ugh," I said, picking up a pen.

"Are you making a list of people we need to interview?" Harold asked.

"Yes," I replied with a snicker. "But I'm pretty sure you mean people I need to interview."

"That's exactly what I meant," Harold said with a chuckle. "Let me know if you need any help or a sounding board."

"Yes, sir," I murmured as I jotted down my notes while Harold and Doctor Wheeler continued to chat.

I wondered if Debbie and Carla knew the big news yet, and I decided the first thing I needed to do was go see them.

"Be back in a bit!" I said as I grabbed my bag and hurried out the door, not bothering with my coat. Debbie's Deliciousness was located one door down on the other side of the flower shop, Sunny Creations.

When I entered the bakery, I stopped short. Usually the place would be packed, but today there were only two customers. Debbie and Carla stood behind the counter, both twiddling their thumbs.

"What's going on?" I whispered over the display case.

"Someone spread the rumor that Lydia Tillwacker died after eating one of my donuts," Debbie said. "I've heard people say that they weren't made right, which made them difficult to swallow, and that I poisoned her. Almost everyone is staying away."

"That's just dumb," I said, rolling my eyes.

"I know."

"Doctor Wheeler was just at my office saying Mrs. Tillwacker was killed. She didn't choke on a donut."

"Oh, my!" Carla exclaimed. "We need details!"

Both women hurried around the counter and pulled me to a table in the corner where they could keep an eye on the store, but also have a private conversation. We always ended up there if no one else occupied it.

"Are you kidding me?" Carla hissed. "Lydia Tillwacker was killed?"

"Yes."

"Oh, thank goodness," Debbie said, bringing her hand to her chest as her shoulders sagged in relief.

"That's not a very nice thing to say," I replied.

Debbie shook her head and shut her eyes for a moment, as if she tried to gather her thoughts. "I don't mean I'm glad she's dead. I'm just glad that no one can speculate about my products and ruin my livelihood. I'm terribly sorry she's gone to meet her maker, rest her soul, but I also don't want to be driven out of business by rumors."

"I get it, Debbie," I said. "I understand. Hopefully once everyone knows the truth, you'll have the usual crowd back."

She sat back in her chair and laced her arms over her chest. "What did Wheeler say? How was she killed?"

"He thinks she was hit on the head from behind."

"With what?" Carla asked.

"Probably something from the fireplace set. That's what he's guessing, anyway. There wasn't any blood."

Debbie furrowed her brow. "How do you know? Did Wheeler tell you about it?"

"No. I found her."

My friends stared at me a moment as if I'd just spoken another language and they were trying to decipher my words.

"Seriously?" Carla asked.

"Yes."

"Oh, my word, Tilly!" Debbie exclaimed. "Was it true she was eating a donut?"

"Yes."

"Are you okay?"

"I guess so," I said with a shrug. "I'm better than I was yesterday."

"What a terrible thing," Carla said.

"Agreed."

"Do you think she did it?" Debbie asked.

I pursed my lips in confusion. "Who?"

"Mrs. Marple."

For a second, I had no idea what she was thinking, but then I remembered Mrs. Marple had been incredibly upset after visiting Lydia.

"She did say she wanted to beat Lydia over the head," Debbie continued. "Maybe she'd been talking literally."

"You're right," I said. "I remember that now that you mention it."

The door chimes rang and Debbie and Carla stood to help Betty Frank, the owner of the Filly Feed, who still hated me for putting her best friend in prison. I doubted she'd ever get over it, but what had she expected me to do. Go down for a crime I didn't commit?

As I waited, I went over our conversation with Mrs. Marple. Yes, she'd been very angry, but had she been mad enough to kill? Over the knitting club, of all things?

After Betty received her coffee and left, they returned to the table. I leaned in and whispered, "Do you think we should tell the sheriff about Mrs. Marple?"

"I don't know," Debbie replied with a shrug. "I honestly can't see her having the physical strength to bash Lydia. She's in her seventies now."

My neighbor, Minnie Johnson, was in her late fifties and did pullups in the barn. Betty Frank, who was even older than Minnie, swung bales of hay around like they were pillows. "Mrs. Marple has lived on a farm her whole life. My guess is that she's very strong. She doesn't look like she sits around and watches television all day long."

"She doesn't seem that tough to me," Carla said, shaking her head.

"Are you kidding me?" I said with a snort. "That woman is fierce under that sweet façade. Remember when she almost got run over before they put in the stoplight? From what I hear, she marched over to the mayor's office and gave him a tongue-lashing that would make a sailor blush."

"Oh, come on," Carla said. "We know how everything gets blown out of proportion around here. I don't think she said all those things that we heard."

"Even if half of it is true, that woman has fortitude and I wouldn't be a bit surprised if Lydia had made her so angry, she slammed her in the back of the head. A heat of the moment crime."

Debbie sighed. "I don't know, Tilly."

"Well, it's something we need to keep in mind, but I don't think we should tell the sheriff. I don't want to throw Mrs. Marple under the proverbial bus."

"If she didn't do it, who did?" Carla asked. "She admitted to being there, and you two say she was madder than a wet cat."

"Carla's got a point," Debbie said. "There was maybe an hour or so between when Mrs. Marple was at the Tillwacker house and when you went there. If she didn't kill her, she was most likely the last one to see her alive."

"You're right," I replied. "I think we need to investigate it. As Mrs. Marple has said, the sheriff's department isn't smart enough to solve a murder. It's above their pay grade."

"But you've solved two, Tilly," Debbie said with a slow grin. "You're intelligent enough, and Carla and I are by your side, reporting for duty."

I nodded and sat back in my chair as a chill spread over my skin. It wouldn't hurt to poke my nose where it didn't belong under the guise of reporting. I'd done it before and it had gone well. I'd solved two murders. I hated to admit it, but I did get a secret thrill when I bested the sheriff and I liked the excitement of the hunt. "Looks like I better get to work. We have a killer to find."

4

I HAD DECIDED to allow the Tillwacker family some time to grieve before I interviewed them. I'd never met Mr. Tillwacker or their messy daughter, but I assumed they'd be terribly upset with Lydia's passing.

From what I'd heard from Mrs. Marple, the knitting club wouldn't be grieving. Since I'd been covering their activities for so long, I'd grown to know some of the members well enough that I felt comfortable calling on them.

Myra Kent had always been very sweet and she'd even knitted me a scarf as a thank you for writing articles about the club. She lived three doors down from Lydia and was my first stop.

The front door to the brown house opened as I

parked my truck. Myra stood at about my height and had an athletic build. Nothing like my neighbor, Minnie, who exercised at least twice a day, but the body of a woman who kept active in her later years. As I approached the stoop, I noted her red eyes, messy brown hair, and puffy face, and she clenched a Kleenex in her palm.

"Hey, Myra," I said as I ascended the stairs. "How are you?"

"Upset," she replied with a sad smile. "Did you hear that Lydia Tillwacker is dead?"

"Yes, and I'm so sorry."

She grabbed my hand and pulled me into an embrace. After a moment she released me and held me at arm's length. "What can I do for you, sweet girl?"

"If you're not too sad, I was hoping we could talk about Lydia."

"Is it for the paper?"

"Yes. I wanted to get some background information and I didn't want to talk to the family quite yet."

"Come in. I just made some coffee."

I followed her through the foyer and down the hallway to the kitchen. As I stood at the counter, I glanced around at the gray and blue wallpaper and black appliances. On the counter, I noted a power bill addressed to Ted and Lydia Tillwacker and figured it had been misdelivered. Oak Peak had suffered issues in the past with the post office.

As Myra poured us both a mug, her grief seemed to radiate off her in waves. It became an almost tangible force in the room and settled heavily in my heart. Myra truly was in deep mourning.

"Let's sit," she said, and we settled across from each other at the kitchen table.

"I'm really sorry for your loss," I began. Interviewing people about the dead never got any easier, and I hoped it never would. I didn't want to become calloused and hard like Harold could be.

"Thanks, Tilly. I'm simply horrified."

"It's hard to imagine someone could do that."

"You know that she was killed then?" Myra asked as she wiped her eyes.

"I found out today."

She shook her head. "Ted, Lydia's husband, told me today as well. Lydia and I had our issues, especially when it came to the knitting club, but I did think of her as my friend. I'll miss her."

What a perfect opening. "Issues with the knitting club?" I asked, feigning ignorance. Mrs. Marple had given me an earful, but it always helped to get a different point of view.

"Yes," Myra said with a sigh. "I'm not sure what got into that woman, but she declared herself the president, had contracts for us all to sign and took out all the fun by pushing us to up our production. It used to be a social event where we'd have a little wine, knit and gossip. A friendly, fun thing for us to do. She ruined the club."

The exact same way Mrs. Marple had described the situation. Myra was obviously upset not only by Lydia's death, but the red tinge in her cheeks spoke anger to me.

"I was supposed to interview her about Cozies for Christmas yesterday. Were you all on board with that project?"

"Absolutely not," Myra stated. "The homeless shelter needs scarves, mittens and blankets far more than the hospital needs baby booties. A lot of us felt we should put our resources where it's most important, but Lydia said it would look better if we did booties."

It was as if I was having the exact same conversation with Mrs. Marple once again.

"Why is that?" I asked.

"Because we can make booties pretty quickly. The other stuff takes longer, and we wouldn't have as many items to present to the homeless shelter as we'd have to give to the hospital if we stuck with covering baby feet. It was all about the number of items we made. In Lydia's mind, the higher amount we could give, the more successful we were as a club. Of course, most of us joined for the social aspect, and it was fun to see our pictures in the paper, but Lydia turned it into a manufacturing line."

A knock on the front door startled me and I turned to see who it could be. Myra stood and hurried down the hallway to answer it. She greeted someone, then two sets of footsteps approached.

Joanne, another member of the knitting club, entered and her eyes widened in surprise when she saw me.

"Joanne, you remember Tilly," Myra said. "She's interviewing me about Lydia."

"May her soul find eternal peace," Joanne said, making the sign of the cross. "It's nice to see you, Tilly."

"You, too. I'm sorry for the loss of your friend."

"Well, I wouldn't really consider her a friend," Joanne said as she sat down and Myra fetched her a cup of coffee. "Not with the way she'd been acting lately."

"Myra was just telling me about that."

"Honestly, I don't know what got into that

woman. She used to be pleasant. Funny. Always smiling. But something happened and it changed her. Probably within the last year or so. Don't you think, Myra?"

"Agreed."

"What do you suppose it was?" I asked.

"I've heard rumors," Joanne said, "but I don't know anything factual."

"What have you heard?" I asked, more curious than anything. I had no intention of printing rumors or gossip, but I did like listening to them.

Joanne leaned toward me. "Her husband was having an affair."

"Let's not speak ill of the dead," Myra scolded. "That's the Devil working within you."

"I'm not talking about Lydia," Joanne said, rolling her eyes. "Her husband, Ted, hasn't passed on, unless something has changed in the past forty-five minutes when I saw him outside fetching the mail."

"it seems wrong to be gossiping about Lydia's husband," Myra said, wringing her hands in her lap. "Can we change the subject?"

"Fine," Joanne huffed. "I've also heard her daughter is on drugs. That's why she moved back home."

"Please!" Myra yelled as she slammed her palm

on the table, causing Joanne and me to startle. "The woman hasn't even been dead for forty-eight hours! Can we give her some peace? Satan is hard at work within you today!"

Joanne glared at Myra for a brief moment. "Satan isn't anywhere near this heart, and how dare you say that to me?" Without another word, she stood and stalked to the front door. The soft click of it closing seemed louder than a slam.

"I'm sorry about that," Myra said as tears welled in her eyes. "I hate gossip, but Joanne thrives on it. Usually, I'm able to keep my lips sealed when she starts up, but Lydia was my friend, and I hate all these rumors. The wound is still too fresh and Lydia isn't here to defend herself or her family."

"Of course," I said, reaching over and squeezing her hand. "Is it true about her daughter being a drug addict? I may know someone who can help."

"I don't know, Tilly," she replied with a sigh. "I've listened to the rumors, but I don't have any idea of what is the truth. The girl is in her early twenties, if I recall correctly. She moved out at eighteen and came back about a year or so ago. I see her every now and then, but she looks completely normal to me."

"What does the gossip mill say about her?"

Myra shook her head as if it pained her to repeat

what she'd heard. "She's a party girl. Always at some bar or another. Can't keep her legs closed, and she's on drugs. Things like that."

"Why did she move home?"

"I don't know. It happened about a year ago and Lydia said Penny, her daughter, couldn't get a job in Los Angeles, so she moved back here. She didn't give a lot of details. Lydia wasn't happy about it, but at the same time, I could tell she was very worried about her daughter. When I tried to question her about it, she became defensive and nasty."

"That's too bad."

"If the girl has a drug problem, I got the feeling Lydia was ashamed of it, when she should have been trying to help her."

Derek and I had talked about attempting to assist people who don't want to be helped and how it was an exercise in futility. He admitted the only thing that had turned him around was his father blaming him for his mother's death. Only then did he want to get help because the guilt weighed so heavily.

"It's such a sad situation over there," Myra said as the tears began to fall again. "Horrible."

I sat with her quietly for a bit longer until she no longer cried.

"Nancy Jones is going to take over the knitting club leadership," Myra said as she wiped her eyes. "The girls wanted me to do it, but I can't without God's blessing, and I just don't feel it. Nancy did tell me she wanted to work with the homeless shelter for Cozies for Christmas. If you'd called before you came, I could have saved you the trip and sent you directly to her. But I do appreciate you sitting with me. I don't think I added much for your article."

"It's not a big deal," I said, getting to my feet. "I'm sorry for your loss, Myra."

"Thank you."

My boots echoed on the hardwood floor as she walked me to the front door.

"Oh! Do you have Nancy's phone number?" I asked.

I couldn't recall meeting the woman, so I definitely wasn't on friendly terms with her. A phone call would be necessary to introduce myself and get her address.

"Yes. Let me jot it down for you."

Myra disappeared into the kitchen again and hurried back moments later, handing me a slip of paper. "Here you go. I'll let her know you'll be calling."

"Thanks."

I trotted down the stairs and slid into my pickup, then pulled away from the curb. What an odd woman. She'd shown me a side of her I hadn't seen before.

Myra may have thought that my visit had been a waste of time, but I'd actually learned quite a bit.

First, if Lydia's daughter, Penny, was indeed a drug addict, could she have been desperate enough to possibly kill her mother? Perhaps for money, or in the heat of an argument? And second, if Ted, the husband, had been having an affair, could it be that the other woman had become so enraged that he was still married, she did away with his wife? Or he'd asked Lydia for a divorce, she'd disagreed, and he'd murdered her?

Then there were the members of the knitting club. None had been too happy with Lydia's leadership, but could one of them have grown so discontented, she'd killed her in a fit of rage?

I'd been investigating Lydia's death for an hour, and I already had more suspects than I could handle.

5

_____

AN HOUR LATER, I sat at my desk staring at the tip of a pencil and waiting for Nancy Jones to return my call while trying to find the gumption to phone Ted Tillwacker and ask if he'd meet with me. I had wanted to give him some time before doing so, but Harold had requested that I interview him right away.

My phone rang, startling me. I picked it up to see it was my mom.

"Hey, Mama!" I said, grinning. "How are you?"

"Tilly! I'm good, honey buns. How are things there in the wild, wild west?"

I rolled my eyes and laughed. "Mama, California isn't the wild west any longer. We're pretty calm and respectable."

"Well, I don't know about that. Hank watches those westerns, and there's nothing respectable about any of it. Gunfights in the streets, prostitution, gambling..."

"Except all that took place a lifetime ago. We don't even ride around in horse drawn carriages any longer."

Mama laughed and my chest tightened. I missed her and was excited for her and Hank to visit at Christmas.

"Two more weeks until you're here!" I said. "I'm excited to see you and I can't wait for you to meet Derek."

"Well, that's what I called about," my mom said, the joy in her voice now gone. "Hank and I aren't going to make it this year."

My heart sank and I closed my eyes. "How come?"

"We just can't afford it, honey. The cost of plane tickets at this time of year is ridiculously expensive. I'm sorry."

"That's okay," I said, trying to remain upbeat, although I could hear that I failed miserably. "I understand."

"You're disappointed," Mom said.

"Well, sure. I haven't seen you two in a long time."

"I know, honey. Tourist season has been slow this year with the hurricane, so Hank's business has taken a hit."

Hank ran swap tours in Louisiana for those who wanted to get up close and personal with gators, and even had one who lived out back of the house he'd named Irwin, after Steve Irwin, the Crocodile Hunter. When the man had died, it was as if Hank had lost his son and had gone into a deep depression that lasted weeks.

"I'm sorry to hear that," I said. "I do wish you could come out, though. I wanted you to meet Derek, Tinker and Belle, and see my house."

"I want that as well, honey, but it's just not going to happen during Christmas. Maybe early next year we can get out there. You know, you're always welcome to come here."

"Okay," I said with a sigh. "I'll give it some thought."

My parents hadn't visited since I'd married Tommy. A lot had changed since then, and I really wanted to show them how good my life had become.

"Tell me what else is going on, Tilly," Mama said, her enthusiasm returning.

I gave her the rundown on Tinker and Belle, and told her about Mrs. Tillwacker.

"Such a shame," she said. "Poor woman. And you finding the body... are you okay, Tilly?"

Was I okay? To a certain extent. I'd feel better once I had found the killer. "Overall, I'm good. Just really busy."

We talked a few more minutes, and then said our goodbyes. I tried not to let the disappointment at them being unable to visit bring me down, so I returned to work with a sigh.

I called Mr. Tillwacker, praying with each ring he wouldn't pick up. I raised my fist in triumph when it went directly to voicemail. "Hello, Mr. Tillwacker. This is Tilly Bordeaux from the Tri-Town Times. First, let me say that I'm so sorry for your loss. I'd met Lydia on a couple different occasions and really liked her. I want to write a few articles about her life and hoped I could interview you and your daughter. Could you please give me a call at your earliest convenience? I would greatly appreciate it."

After giving my number, I set down the phone. It had been much easier to leave a message and tell him what I wanted than to speak to him about it. If it weren't for Harold breathing down my neck, I'd definitely would have given him a few more days before approaching him.

Spinning around in my chair, I stared at the

window. The residents of Oak Peak bustled around Oak Peak Avenue, the main drag of our little town. Some carried bags of purchases, which I assumed to be Christmas gifts.

Speaking of which, I had no idea what to get Derek. Since it was just going to be the two of us, I wanted the day to be special, but I was still at a loss at what my present to him should be. He had everything and money to buy anything he wanted.

Harold hurried in. "How are things going, Tilly?" he asked, his voice harried and out of breath. "It's cold out. Damn snow. There's a crash on the freeway between Cedarville and Little River involving four cars. It's closed. Can you call the Department of Transportation and get the details? Then call the sheriff's office and see about casualties and fatalities?"

I placed the phone calls and wrote up a quick piece with the information I'd received, then emailed it to Harold. Thankfully, no one had been seriously hurt, but two people were in the hospital with minor injuries and expected to make a full recovery. I made a note on my calendar to call the hospital tomorrow for an update.

"What's going on with the Lydia Tillwacker murder?" Harold asked a few moments later. He sat with his back to me as he stared at his computer screen reading the piece I'd just sent him.

"I'm waiting on phone calls from her husband and from the new president of the knitting club."

Harold turned to face me. "If you haven't heard back from the widower in an hour, place another call."

"I don't want to harass him," I replied. "I mean, his wife just died yesterday. I'm sure I'm the last person he wants to talk to."

"That may be, but we need to stay on top of the news."

"Harold, it's not like someone is going to swipe the story out from under us," I said. "This isn't Los Angeles. We're the only paper that serves the Tri-Town area."

"Yes, and we want to keep it that way. If someone sees that we're lazy or not keeping the public informed, they could come in and we'll have competition. I don't want that."

He turned back to his computer and I sighed again, this time in frustration. There was a fine line between being a reporter and being a decent human being. I'd wait until I heard from Mr. Tillwacker instead of pestering the man.

I turned back to the window and stared out at

the busy street once again and wondered when the next wave of snow would hit. Hopefully, we'd get a day or two of reprieve and I made a mental note to check on the weather when I got home.

Our office sat right across from the hardware store. Jumping to my feet, I ran outside when I saw Derek emerge from there.

I waved as we stood on opposite sides of the street waiting for the light to change. Then I could hurry through the parked cars to him.

Once the light changed, we both stepped into the street and met halfway.

"I was coming to meet you!" I exclaimed, grabbing his hand.

"Let's get back to your side," Derek said. When we were safely out of traffic, he leaned over and gave me a kiss. "How's my favorite reporter today?"

"I'm fine. Harold's on my nerves a bit, but overall, I'm good. What are you doing at the hardware store?"

"Buying stuff to put up Christmas lights on your house. I thought it would be fun with your parents coming."

I stared at him a beat, so touched by the thought, I couldn't speak. Did this man's niceties know no bounds?

"If you don't think it's a good idea, I won't do put

them up," he said, his smile fading. "I thought it would be fun. My dad used to decorate the house when we were little, and it always helped put our family in the spirit. But like I said, if you—˘

"No, Derek. I think it sounds great. I appreciate the offer, and yes, I'd love for you put lights on the house. But my parents aren't coming."

"Why is that?" he asked, his brow furrowed. "When did you find out?"

"Just a little while ago. My mom called and said they can't afford to come out this year. Maybe in the spring, but not for Christmas. I guess the tourists aren't flocking to Louisiana this year, and Hank's business isn't doing as well as usual."

"I'm sorry about that Tilly," Derek, said, pulling me in for a hug. "I know you were really looking forward to it."

As I lay my head on his chest, I smiled. Yes, I was disappointed that my parents weren't coming, but I was so thrilled with my relationship with Derek, it drowned out some of my sorrow. "They said we could come out there if we wanted."

"Do you want to do that? I can look into tickets this afternoon if you do."

I stepped back and shook my head. "What would I do with Tinker, Belle, and the chickens? I don't like the idea of someone coming into the house to watch them."

"What about Debbie? Or Carla?"

"Debbie's going to her sister's in Oregon and Carla and Mac live too far away. I wouldn't feel comfortable asking them."

"You're probably right," he said with a nod.

"Tilly!" Harold called from the front door to the office. "Your phone's ringing! It might be Tillwacker!"

"I've got to go," I said to Derek as I stood on my tiptoes and gave him a kiss.

"Okay, love you."

"Love you, too."

I hurried back into the office feeling much better after my visit with Derek. The first time he'd told me he loved me was in the hospital after he'd proposed to me at the Halloween dance where I'd vomited on him and then passed out. We seemed to do everything backwards—one would think he would tell me he loved me before asking for my hand in marriage. Yet, it didn't matter. I was happy, and he frequently expressed the same to me. We may not do things in the traditional order, but we did them our way, and everything seemed to be working out just fine.

After picking up my phone, I noted that Nancy

Jones had called, not Ted Tillwacker. Harold stared at me expectantly.

"It's the president of the knitting club," I said.

His shoulders sagged and he returned to his desk, muttering something under his breath.

Ignoring him, I made my call. Harold's shoulders slumped in disappointment as he sat down; however, I knew that Nancy could be a wealth of information on solving Lydia's murder, and I made an appointment to stop by later that afternoon.

6

—————

Nancy Jones lived on the other side of town from
the Tillwackers, but the houses were almost carbon
copies. I stared at the addresses of the neat, tidy rows
of homes lining both sides of the street and pulled
over to the curb when I found Nancy's.

After locking the truck, I shoved my hands into
my parka and strode up the cement walkway, careful
about where I stepped in case ice had formed under
the blasts of cold wind. The sun was shining, but if I
was a betting woman, I'd place my money on the
temperature hovering right around thirty degrees.

The door opened before I could knock. The
woman was my height and maybe in her fifties with
brown hair and blue eyes that glittered under the
sunlight. I recognized her from my interactions with

the club, but I could never recall us speaking. If I remembered correctly, Nancy had always been quiet and hadn't participated in the chatter much.

"Tilly?" she asked with a grin. "I'm Nancy. Please come in."

I stepped into her warm home and slid out of my coat, then hung it on a peg. "Thank you for returning my call so soon."

"Of course. Let's go into the kitchen. I'm looking forward to setting the record straight on the knitting club."

I followed her down the hall, unsure of what she meant. What record?

She led me into the tidy black and tan kitchen and motioned for me to sit down at the table. "Would you like some coffee, Tilly?"

"That would be great. Thank you."

A beige tabby cat walked around the corner and stood in the entryway, eyeing me suspiciously.

I patted my leg and smiled. It sauntered over and rubbed against my shin and meowed.

"Meet Brownie," Nancy said as she poured. "He's friendly once he gets to know you."

As he continued to smell my shoe and snuggle his head against me, I imagined Belle wouldn't be too happy with me when I arrived home and she caught his scent. I allowed him to sniff my hand and once I had passed his test, he jumped up on my lap and settled in, purring loudly.

"He sure took to you fast," Nancy said as she set down our mugs, then took a seat. "He's usually wary of strangers."

"He must sense I'm an animal person. I've got a dog, a cat, and a couple of chickens."

Granted, I wasn't too fond of the chickens, but Tinker was, so I kept them.

I sipped my coffee and stroked the cat, then grinned at the perfect moment. Coffee and cats. Was there anything better?

My dog would probably have something to say about that.

"So you're here to talk about the knitting club?" Nancy asked.

I nodded and focused my attention on her instead of the feline in my lap. "Yes. I spoke to Myra Kent and she said you would be taking over as president of the club."

"That's correct. Some of the girls wanted her to do it, but she said she's too distraught. I volunteered."

"How nice of you to step in."

"It had to be done," Nancy said, rolling her eyes. "The club is being run into the ground. I had numerous discussions with Lydia about her leadership skills, or I should say, her lack thereof, and I'm looking forward to taking the club and its members in a different direction."

I retrieved my notebook from my purse in an effort to hide my surprise while trying not to disturb Brownie, who now slept soundly. The drama surrounding the club never failed to shock me. What should have been a bunch of ladies sitting around making cute things and socializing seemed to have a very sinister underbelly.

"What was wrong with Lydia's leadership?" I asked.

"She ran the club like a dictator," Nancy replied. "Talking about meeting quotas and really getting angry at those who didn't. I tried to explain to her the philosophy of catching more flies with honey than with vinegar, but she wouldn't listen. I even offered to take over the club from her just to try to save it, but no... she wouldn't do that either."

"You offered to basically take her position?"

"Exactly. Things are going to be much better now I'm in charge. Much different."

"How is that?" I asked.

"Well, for starters, we're going to have a Facebook group. Eventually, I imagine taking the club nationwide. I'm going to call it Nancy's Knitters for Mankind."

Pursing my lips together, I jotted down the notes. Sounded like Nancy was a bit full of herself.

"Can you imagine?" she continued. "Women from all over the country working together for one great cause. It will be magical. Perhaps if it becomes popular enough, I can take Nancy's Knitters worldwide!"

The woman was excited about her plans of world domination over knitting clubs. I gave her points for her enthusiasm and drive, but it struck me as odd because she'd always been so quiet.

"Don't write anything about the Facebook group and my ideas quite yet," she said, laying her palm over my pen. "I haven't talked to the girls yet. I'd hate for them to read about it in the paper before I had the chance to share my vision. I'm going to call a meeting to let them know."

"I won't say anything," I replied with a nod and removed my hand from under hers. "How will your leadership be different from Lydia's? You're going to need a lot of group participation to reach your vision."

"I know," she said, a sly smile spreading over her

face. "I can be very persuasive in getting people to do what I want."

Nancy seemed harmless enough, but something about her smile gave me the willies. She reminded me of an evil Cheshire cat.

"Well, should definitely be interesting to see where this leads," I said, then took a sip of coffee. "Tell me about your plans for the Christmas project."

"We're definitely going to make items for the homeless shelter. I envision scarves, mittens and some blankets. Of course, we'll need the paper to cover our donation with an article and pictures."

"Christmas is only a couple weeks away," I said. "When are you planning on presenting the items to the shelter?"

"Oh, Christmas Day, for sure. It will be a wonderful gesture and I can't wait to see the joy we bring those in need."

I truly believed in helping others, but I also wondered how the members of the knitting club would feel about being asked to spend a few hours of Christmas Day at the homeless shelter instead of being home with their families. Some would probably be fine with it, but others would be angry it was being asked of them.

"Well, we may need to do some photos before-hand. A lot of people have plans on Christmas Day," I said with a smile, trying to hide my irritation with the woman. I planned on snuggling up with Derek, Tinker and Belle watching Christmas movies, maybe have a little eggnog, stay my pajamas and not leave the house. I worked hard and deserved Christmas to myself.

"Well, that throws a bit of a wrench in my plans," Nancy said. She studied her coffee and chewed her lip for a moment. "But I suppose we can compromise. Perhaps we can make our donation with the paper covering it on Christmas Eve?"

That was doubtful as well. Since Harold would be leaving town for the holiday, that left me alone to run everything, meaning I would need to be available Christmas Eve to take the pictures at the homeless shelter. Call me selfish, but I didn't know if I was ready to give up my first Christmas with Derek.

"We'll see," I said. "Just out of curiosity, when did you approach Lydia about your plans of taking over the knitting club from her?"

"Oh, almost from the beginning when she whipped out those stupid contracts. But she wouldn't budge."

"How many times did you bring it up with her?"

"Oh, gosh. I don't know. Numerous times."

I stroked Brownie, who still lay in my lap, and I wondered what persuasion skills she'd used to get her way. They'd obviously failed with Lydia.

The more I talked with Nancy, the more I felt as if she had tried to pressure Lydia to make the changes she desired, not what the group wanted. From what I'd heard from Mrs. Marple and Myra, most of the members wanted to sit around, drink wine, and knit. They weren't looking for a regimented club. Lydia hadn't realized it, and neither did Nancy.

"Well, I better be heading out," I said, slowly standing and lifting the snoozing kitty from my thighs. I set him down on the chair and he glared at me, but then curled up and went back to sleep. "I appreciate your time."

"Of course, dear. As Christmas draws closer, I'll be in touch about having you meet us at the homeless shelter in Cedarville for the photos."

I smiled but didn't commit. I'd have to think that one over and talk about it with Derek. Chances were good I'd be offering Nancy another option, and I could already tell she wouldn't be happy.

We said our goodbyes while I slipped on my coat, and I carefully walked to my truck.

Driving home, I couldn't help but really think

about Nancy. She had big plans for the knitting club, but she had never seemed that outgoing and gregarious to me. Honestly, I'd never noticed her before. There were some big personalities in the group, and they always stood out to me, or I knew the women from around town, which was the case with Mrs. Marple.

Nancy hadn't pulled those plans out of thin air. She'd been pressuring Lydia for a long time to see her way of thinking, and Lydia had pushed back, which Nancy obviously hadn't appreciated.

The woman was now in the position she'd coveted for quite a while. I'd never imagined her being so pushy, but she'd admitted she'd been with Lydia, and she'd given me a little taste of it as well by insisting I work over Christmas.

My stepfather, Hank, always told me that it was the quiet ones that needed to be watched the most. One time, when I'd been about fifteen, he'd taken me out on the boat deep into the swamps. He'd turned off the engine and we floated in the quiet waters. Birds called from the trees and insects buzzed all around us, but the stillness of the swamp settled around us like a heavy, wet blanket.

Hank had pointed to a gator submerged under the water with nothing but his eyes revealed near the shore. If he hadn't shown me exactly where to find the gator, I'd never would have seen him.

"The quiet ones, the still ones," he'd whispered. "Those are the ones you never see coming, and they'll bite off your face before you even know they're on you. That goes for animals and humans alike. Remember that, Tilly. Always watch the quiet ones."

Was Nancy like the submerged gator? Had she waited patiently and killed Lydia Tillwacker when she couldn't get what she wanted?

She was definitely one to keep on my radar.

7

My dreams had been filled with talking alligators
that sounded exactly like Nancy, softly telling me
that if I didn't do as they said, they'd stab me with a
knitting needle. When I woke, I felt like I'd ran all
night long instead of getting eight hours of sleep.

Derek wasn't in bed, which didn't surprise me
because he rose very early. While I stood and
stretched, I gazed over at his home and noted a light
dusting of snow had appeared overnight. It had been
a good two months since Derek had spent the night
in his house, and I wondered if we should just live
together. He ran over there daily to grab the mail
and turn on the faucets to make sure the pipes
hadn't frozen, but it seemed silly to keep two houses
when we spent all our time at mine. I'd have to think

it over and decide what to do. Having him formally move in was a big step, but we were already cohabitating. We'd simply be making a permanent arrangement.

After slipping on my robe, I walked down the stairs, each one creaking beneath my weight. Being an older house, this was to be expected. I thought I heard Derek whispering, but when I rounded the corner, I found him sitting on the couch with Belle on his lap. Perhaps he'd been talking to her.

"Good morning, beautiful," he said with a smile. "The coffee is made and the chickens have been fed."

"Oh, wow. Thank you."

I stumbled into the kitchen and pulled a mug from the cabinet, then poured myself a cup. Derek came up behind me and circled his arms around my waist. "Did you sleep well?"

"No," I muttered. "I had some crazy dreams."

"I'm sorry to hear that," he said, his voice laced with concern. "Would breakfast make you feel better?"

"Oh, most certainly," I replied with a smile. "Thank you."

I sat at the kitchen table as Derek prepared eggs and bacon. "Were you talking to someone when I came down the stairs?"

Derek glanced at me with a grin turning his lips. "If you count Belle as someone, then yes."

"Oh, she's definitely a someone," I said, eyeing my cat who perched on the corner of the counter.

"We were discussing our plans for the day."

"And what are those, if I may ask?"

"I'm putting up the Christmas lights. Belle said she'd love to supervise me from inside."

I laughed as he handed me a loaded plate, then sat down with his own. "This looks great. Thank you."

"What are you up to today?" Derek asked in between bites.

"Ugh. I have to call Ted Tillwacker again and ask for an interview. Harold is really on me about that. But I think there's a fine line between doing my job and being a decent human being, especially when it comes to murder."

"Speaking of which," Derek said, "are you looking for who did it?"

"Who did what?" I asked, hoping that if I played stupid, he'd drop the subject.

Derek sighed loudly. "Tilly, don't play dumb. Are you looking for who killed Mrs. Tillwacker?"

I wanted to lie but I couldn't. Not to Derek. "Carla and Debbie are asking around about it. If I happen to stumble across who did it while interviewing those involved, then I'll turn everything over to the idiot sheriff."

"Please be careful, okay? Don't do anything stupid that may put you in danger."

With a grin, I nodded. He worried about me, and I appreciated it, but I also liked how he refrained from telling me I couldn't do what I wanted. My ex would have done that—just flat out told me no, I wouldn't be looking for a killer. Not on his watch.

"I better get dressed," I said, standing. "Thank you for breakfast and for supporting me."

"Of course I support you, silly," he replied. "I'll take care of the dishes and feed Tinker."

"Is she out with her chickens?"

"Yes. As soon as the sun rose, she bolted."

"She's something else," I replied. "I'd love to hear her thoughts on the hens. Why does she like them so much? I personally think they're mean."

"They probably sense your hatred and feel threatened. Then, they attack."

"Really? Do you think that's it?"

"I don't know, Tilly. I don't speak chicken."

We both laughed as I headed upstairs to get ready. A half-hour later, I kissed Derek at the door and we made plans for lunch.

"Be careful up on the ladder," I said. "I'd rather have zero Christmas lights and you in one piece."

"I'll be fine," he replied. "How about you be careful while searching for a murderer?"

Well, he had me there. "Fair enough. I'll see you soon."

Thankfully, the snow hadn't stuck to the roads, and my drive into town went by without issue.

I parked in front of the paper and headed into Debbie's to check in. Once again, I found the bakery almost empty. Debbie stood frozen behind the counter like a deer in headlights, her eyes wide.

"What's going on?" I said as I approached her. "Where is everyone?"

"They think my donuts killed Lydia Tillwacker!" Debbie hissed. "I can't believe this!"

I glanced around the store once more. "We published the article that she'd been murdered with a weapon. I don't get it."

"This is going to ruin me," Debbie said. "All these people who think the local gossip is gospel and actually take everything so seriously... I don't know what I'm going to do!"

Pursing my lips, I didn't bother to remind her that she was the heartbeat of the gossip vine in our small town. She was upset, and I didn't want to throw gas on the fire. "It'll blow over," I said. "I'm sure of it. Give people a few days, and they'll be back. Your goodies are too yummy for them to stay away for long."

"Thank you for saying that," Debbie said. "I just hope you're right. Do you want coffee?"

I nodded as the door chimes rang. Both of us turned to find Mrs. Marple shuffling in. She waved and came right over. "Are you girls having coffee?"

"Yes," I replied. "Do you want to join us?"

"I'd love to." She glanced over her shoulder then whispered, "I have some news."

"Do you want the usual, Mrs. Marple?" Debbie asked.

"Yes, please, dear. And if you have any brandy, put a shot of that in there as well."

"It's nine in the morning!" Debbie shrieked.

"If you'd have the morning I've had, you'd be hitting the bottle as well."

"You two have a seat," Debbie said, shaking her head. "I'll bring everything right over."

"What happened?" I asked once Mrs. Marple and I were seated.

"Let's wait until Debbie joins us, if you don't mind," she answered, slipping off her coat. "I don't like repeating myself."

I studied the older woman. Bags hung under her eyes and her mouth pinched in worry.

"I don't have any brandy, but here's some Kahlúa," Debbie said. "It's all I have."

"That will do." Mrs. Marple poured some into her coffee. "I prefer brandy, but I'm not going to be picky."

Debbie and I exchanged worried glances and waited for the older woman to speak. My gut twisted in anxiety. Whatever she had to share, it was bound to be bad news.

Mrs. Marple took a couple sips of her drink and licked her lips. "Oh, that's tasty. It hits the spot."

"Don't keep us waiting any longer," Debbie said. "Tell us what happened that requires liquor before noon."

"Well, I spent the morning with that no-brain idiot, the sheriff."

I groaned and rolled my eyes. "Why? What did he say?"

"He asked me if I killed Lydia Tillwacker!"

Debbie gasped and brought her hand to her mouth. "How did he even know you were at her house?"

"Well, at first, I thought you two may have said something to him. But then he told me that the

Tillwackers have one of those fancy-pants doorbells that videotapes people. They looked over the footage and saw me. Apparently, I was the last one to see her alive."

The sheriff's timeline matched up with what Debbie and I had thought. Mrs. Marple had been at the house, then I found the body.

"He's coming to talk to you as well, Tilly," Mrs. Marple said. "You're on the footage about an hour after me."

"Great," I said, lacking any enthusiasm. He'd already accused me of murder once. Why not twice?

"Anyway, it wasn't that I minded being questioned," Mrs. Marple said. "I didn't do anything, and my conscience is clean. He's such an incompetent boob, and I'm too old to tolerate idiocy. I don't have the patience for it any longer."

I was almost half her age, and I didn't either.

"Anyway," she continued, "Sheriff Connor was rude and condescending to me until I reminded him that my ancestors founded this town and I didn't appreciate his tone. He straightened up after that, but I can't believe he's still sheriff after bungling not one, but two murders! Nothing but a disgrace, if you ask me."

"I'm not aware of anyone who voted for him,"

Debbie said. "He should have been investigated for voter fraud."

"I tried," I said. "Harold wouldn't allow me to look into it."

Mrs. Marple sipped more of her coffee. "Anyway, he's coming for you next, Tilly. Somehow, someone got into the house between the time I left and when you arrived."

"And there's nothing on the footage that the doorbell captured?" I asked.

"Nothing."

"Which means someone must have been aware of the doorbell and gotten into the house another way," Debbie said. "Unless one of you did off her and you're lying about it."

Mrs. Marple and I glanced at each other and burst out laughing.

"I didn't think so," Debbie said with a grin.

"Well, I better get to work," I said, standing. "Thanks for the warning, Mrs. Marple."

"Of course, dear. Glad to help."

As I strode to the door, I remembered Nancy Jones had said she would be calling a meeting of the knitting club. "Have you heard from Nancy?" I asked Mrs. Marple.

She turned and nodded. "I have. She wanted to

have a meeting tonight. I told her I was busy. I think I'm done with the knitting club for now. It's left a sour taste in my mouth."

"It's probably a good thing to take a break from it," I said. I couldn't imagine Mrs. Marple wanting anything to do with Nancy's grand master plans of world domination on knitting clubs. The woman was like Hitler in her quest. Nazi Nancy of Knitting. She'd just earned herself a new nickname.

I snickered and waved as I left. Just before I opened the door to the Tri-Town Times, my phone buzzed in my pocket. I pulled it out and answered.

"Hey, Byron. How are things going?"

"I was going to call today and tell you that Lydia Tillwacker was murdered, but I see you already have that information." Paper rustled in the background. "Do you mind telling me who your source is?"

"Yes, I do mind," I said, marching into the office. "I can't reveal sources, Byron."

Harold's head jerked up when he heard me, and he stared at me over his glasses.

I wasn't about to let Byron know Harold had a strong relationship with Doctor Wheeler and that he came to us with information right after he informed the police.

"Tilly, if there's a leak in our department, we need to stop it."

"Well, I'm sorry, but reporters do not disclose their sources." I dropped my bag next to my desk and sat in my chair. I glanced at the coffee pot and noted it was full. Did I need another cup? "Is there anything else I can do for you, Byron?"

"Yes," he said. "You can come down to the station. We need to interview you about the murder."

Although I had known it was coming, my stomach churned with nerves. Nope. No more coffee for me. "When do you want me there?"

"As soon as you can."

I hadn't even turned on my computer, so it seemed like a good time. "I'll be right over."

With a sigh, I shoved my phone back in my pocket.

"Where are you going, Tilly?" Harold asked.

"I have to go to the station. Apparently, the sheriff thinks either Mrs. Marple killed Lydia Tillwacker, or I did."

"Did you?" he asked, a smile tugging at his lips.

"Of course not," I replied. "I'll be back later."

As I walked over to the city hall, I called Derek. He didn't answer, so I left a message.

"Hey. The sheriff wants to talk to me about Lydia

Tillwacker's murder. According to Mrs. Marple, he thinks either she or I did it. Can you call your lawyer and have him meet me there? This guy is dumb enough and hates me enough to put me in jail and throw away the key."

8

———

BEFORE ENTERING the sheriff's office, I took a few deep breaths and prepared for battle, wishing I carried a sword. Not that I would use it, but it would empower and embolden me. Really though, who was I kidding? I'd probably chop off my own leg trying to wield it.

The woman at the front desk greeted me, and I waited in the stark lobby. Taking stock of my emotions, I realized I wasn't afraid or nervous, but more angry than anything. I hoped I could keep my irritation under wraps. It was probably a good thing I didn't have a sword or I may stab someone besides myself in my fury.

Byron came through the locked door and motioned me to follow him. He smiled, and that put me at ease a little. I followed him and noted his shoulders looked wider to me. Was it a new uniform, or had he been working out more than usual?

He led me into an interrogation room and shut the door once I'd taken a seat. "I'm going to be conducting the interview today," he said, placing his notebook on the table. "The sheriff has other business."

"That's fine," I replied, feeling a bit mouthy because I shouldn't even be questioned. "I understand why he doesn't want to see me."

Byron furrowed his brow. "And why is that?"

"Because I solved two murders and he didn't," I said with a shrug. "And he's obviously barking up the wrong tree with this one."

"Do you think he's embarrassed or something?"

"Maybe. If I were him, I sure would be."

"Okay, well, you're wrong and I have to say, a little bit full of yourself, Tilly. It doesn't suit you."

Like I cared. I'd rather be angry and generate overconfidence than to be afraid and trembling in my chair.

"So, what did you want to ask me, Byron?" I figured it would be best to move past the discussion on how I was a pro at solving murders and the sheriff wasn't.

"Well, we've got footage from the doorbell. There are two people who entered the house: you and Mrs. Marple. Then, you called 9-1-1."

"And?"

"That means that there's a possibility that you or Mrs. Marple committed the crime."

"Byron, the house has a back door, right? The answer is yes, in case you didn't know. I recall seeing it in the kitchen. The killer could have come in through there. Was it locked when you investigated the murder? If so, that means Mrs. Tillwacker knew her killer and let him in. If not, someone broke in, and I'm assuming there'd be evidence of that on the door. Unless, of course, she was home with the door open, which is also a possibility. We do live in a small town where most people feel safe enough to leave their doors unlocked during the day."

Byron paled as he stared at me. Had they really not considered any of it?

I sighed and crossed my arms over my chest. "Mrs. Marple went to talk to Lydia about the knitting club, as did I. She wasn't happy with the way things were being run, which I'm sure she told you. Lydia asked me to stop by so she could tell me about the knitting club's Christmas project. Neither of us have any interest in killing her. We have no reason to!"

"We're looking into all facets of the investigation," Byron said as he jotted some notes. "Can you go over what happened that morning one last time for me?"

I repeated the story and when I finished, Byron simply stared at me.

"What?" I asked bringing my hand to my face. Did I have something stuck to my cheek? Or did he not believe me? Had I said something to incriminate myself?

"You look so pretty today," Byron said, his voice low and filled with something resembling regret.

"T-Thank you," I stuttered. The conversation had sure taken a turn I hadn't expected.

"Tilly, I just can't sit back and watch you make this mistake with Derek," Byron said. "I know he's living with you now. You're in for a world of hurt."

I narrowed my gaze on him. "Did you bring me in to discuss my love life, or the murder?"

"Both. I want you to give us another chance. We belong together. Please, Tilly."

Pursing my lips, I shook my head. "I've already told you numerous times it's not going to work out between us."

"Tilly, please," he begged. "I can make you happy."

"If you don't have anything else to ask me about

Mrs. Tillwacker, I'd like to go," I said, standing. "This is highly inappropriate, Byron."

The door swung open and I gasped as a giant, bald man dressed in a suit carrying a briefcase strode in, followed by Derek.

"This interview is over," the man said. "I'm Steven Blackburn, Ms. Bordeaux's attorney. She won't be answering any further questions today. If you'd like to continue the interview, you can contact my office to make arrangements."

At right around six-foot-eight and a wall of muscle, the attorney looked more like a linebacker than a legal expert. His sheer size intimidated me, but thankfully, he was on my side.

As Mr. Blackburn laid his business card on the table, Derek hurried over to me and wrapped his arm around my shoulder. Byron stared at the card for a moment, then turned his gaze to Derek. Neither tried to hide the anger and hatred they shared for each other.

"Let's go," Mr. Blackburn commanded.

I didn't dare argue with the man. Glancing over my shoulder, I saw Byron staring at me with longing in his gaze. The fact that he had yet to get over me sort of gave me the creeps.

"Are you okay?" Derek asked quietly as we walked through the lobby.

"I'm fine." But honestly, I wasn't. My overconfidence had fled. The fact Byron wouldn't let go of the fantasy of us being together upset me. What would it take? Did I need to become nasty to him and tell him I found him stupid and boring? How many times had I told him things between us just wouldn't work?

"Did he accuse you of murder?" Mr. Blackburn asked once we were outside, his hard, brown gaze burrowing into me, making me feel even smaller than my five-foot-two stature. "I need to know everything that was said." He pulled out his phone. "I'm going to record this conversation so I have it for my records if it's okay with you, Ms. Bordeaux."

"That's fine," I replied, glad he represented me, but I still found him menacing.

He cleared his throat and spoke into the phone. "December tenth, eleven-forty in the morning. I've just retrieved Matilda Bordeaux from the police station where she was asked to come in and talk to a deputy regarding the murder of Lydia Tillwacker. This serves as record of her conversation with said deputy for the files. Ms. Bordeaux, please tell me about your discussion with the deputy. What's his name?"

"Byron Mills," I replied.

"Excellent. Please go on."

Derek held my hand while I repeated the conversation I'd had with Byron, except I left out the part where he brought up our non-existent relationship. Derek would be upset if he knew the deputy was still pining for me, and I didn't want that. In the end, my heart belonged to Derek, and Byron could do nothing to change it. Why bring the drama into our lives?

"That's it," I said once I'd finished. "It was a short conversation."

Mr. Blackburn nodded and turned off the recorder. "If you think of anything else, please call me. If they ask you back in to talk about the murder, do not step foot inside that building without me by your side, Ms. Bordeaux. Do you understand?"

I nodded and stuck out my hand. "Thank you very much for coming," I said. "I appreciate it, and if I remember anything else, I'll be sure to call you."

The lawyer took my palm in his, his handshake firm. "You're lucky I was in this neck of the woods today visiting another client, or it would have taken me a couple hours to get here. Glad to be of service to you."

He nodded at Derek, then hurried over to a black Mercedes parked in the lot and drove away.

"Thanks for calling him," I said as I wrapped my arms around Derek's waist. "I'm glad you two got here so fast."

"Of course. When I heard your message, I was scared to death they were going to lock you up."

"I know. I was a little concerned about that as well."

He released me and kissed my forehead. "Things worked out for the best, and that's what's important."

"How are the Christmas lights looking?" I asked.

"Not too shabby, if I do say so myself," Derek said as we made our way back to my office. "Not too bad at all."

"I can't wait to see them! Hank used to put up Christmas lights when I lived in Louisiana, but I haven't had any since."

"This Christmas is going to be great!" he exclaimed, squeezing my shoulders.

His enthusiasm rubbed off on me and I smiled. Yes, I was looking forward to the holiday, but the small pit of despair caused by my parents not coming still hung burrowed in my chest.

"I better head home," he said when we arrived in front of the Tri-Town Times. "Unless you have time for lunch."

"Considering I've been out of the office all morning, I should get some work done," I replied. Being summoned to the sheriff's office had really ruined my plans for the day.

Derek leaned in and gave me a quick kiss. "I understand. I'll see you when you get home."

I watched as he strode over to his SUV, then slid in. He waved as he pulled away from the curb.

With a sigh, I opened the office door, wishing I could have gone with him.

"Everything go okay at the sheriff's?" Harold asked.

"It was a quick discussion because Derek showed up with his lawyer. They got me out of there pretty quickly."

"Did you learn anything new?"

Pursing my lips, I considered his question for a moment. I'd learned that Byron still liked me, despite me telling him many times that we weren't going to be together. That was perhaps the most unsettling part.

"No, I replied. "Nothing new."

As I sat down at my desk, I wondered if Byron

had brought me in the station under the pretense of discussing the murder to actually share his feelings. We'd barely discussed the Tillwacker case at all, yet he had seemed flustered when I mentioned someone could have come in through the back door —almost as if he hadn't given it any thought.

"Have you heard back from Tillwacker?" Harold asked. "We really need to interview him."

"I'll call again right now."

As the ringing tone started, I prayed he didn't answer.

"Hello?" a deep voice said.

Dang it!

"Mr. Tillwacker, this is Tilly Bordeaux. I called before and left a message."

"Yes. I was going to phone you today and I'm sorry I haven't called sooner. I'm happy to meet you. Can you come by about three?"

I hadn't expected him to be so kind or accommodating. "Y-yes," I stuttered. "That will be fine. I'll be there at three."

"Great. I look forward to seeing you then."

"Good job, Tilly," Harold said as I set down my phone. "I look forward to reading your article on the family."

Something seemed off to me, but I couldn't place

what it was. Although the man's wife had just died days earlier, he was so calm. Yet, Sophia, Jake Martinez's daughter, had been the same way: focused and determined to run her restaurant.

Perhaps I'd see another side to Ted Tillwacker when I met him and I simply couldn't gauge his grief over the phone.

Unless he was happy his wife was gone, and he'd killed her.

9

———

WHEN I PULLED up in front of the Tillwackers, I was happy to see their steps had been cleared of snow, meaning I wouldn't take a tumble because of ice, but I couldn't rule out a fall due to lack of coordination or tripping over air, as I tended to do.

Nerves tickled my belly as I rang the doorbell. I reminded myself I had thought Sophia Martinez's actions following her dad's death were strange and she hadn't been a murderer.

A tall, thin man dressed in black slacks and a yellow sweater opened the door and greeted me with a sad smile. "Tilly?"

"Yes."

"Come on in."

As he led me into the kitchen, I glanced into the

living room, where I'd discovered Lydia. Everything was in its place, except the fireplace set was missing. My gaze settled on where I'd found her and I couldn't tell anyone had died there.

"Would you like something to drink?" Ted asked.

"No," I replied, sitting at the kitchen table. "I'm fine. I won't take up too much of your time."

"Penny!" he yelled. "Come down here, please!"

Footsteps sounded from the second floor and a moment later, a beautiful young woman appeared in the doorway. Long, blonde hair framed her thin face, and her wide blue eyes studied me closely. I wondered if the family knew I was the one who had found Lydia. I kind of doubted it unless the sheriff's office had informed them, and I wrestled with whether I should disclose the information or not.

"Penny, this is Tilly from the paper," Ted said. "She's writing an article on your mother, and I'd like you to give your input."

I studied her closely as she took the chair opposite of me. Rumor had it she was on drugs, and if that were the case, she was on my list of suspects. She could have killed her mother for any number of reasons, including money or rage if they'd had an argument.

She met my stare and I smiled. Her eyes looked

clear, yet sad. Her skin was flawless and her thick hair was brushed, yet she was painfully thin. I wasn't sure what to look for to determine if someone was on drugs besides what I'd seen of the super hardcore users—horrible skin, missing teeth, cloudy eyes—and Penny looked healthy. If I had to guess, I'd say she was clean.

Ted also sat down while sipping on a glass of water. "What can we do for you, Tilly?"

"Well, first I wanted to say how sorry I am for your loss. Lydia was a very kind person and I liked her a lot. I'd spoken with her quite a few times about the knitting club."

Ted nodded, but Penny rolled her eyes. Did she disagree her mother was a nice person?

"Anyway, I'm writing a series of articles about Lydia's death and I wanted to interview you about her... get a feel for her and her family."

Ted exchanged glances with Penny, but then nodded. "Okay, what did you want to know?"

"Where did you and Lydia meet?" I asked.

"We met when I moved here," Ted replied. "Right out of college, I was offered a job at the accounting firm I currently work for, which was owned by a friend of my father's. Lydia came in one day to have her taxes done, and we began dating."

"So how long were you married before she passed?" I asked. Math had never been my strong suit, and I wanted to be certain I had the numbers correct.

He glanced over at Penny and laid a hand over her forearm. "Thirty years."

I studied Ted's daughter. He seemed to be in his late fifties, perhaps sixties. If that were the case, that meant they'd waited a few years before conceiving Penny. She didn't look a day over twenty-five.

"Did Lydia work outside the house?" I asked.

Ted shook his head. "We believed in a more traditional home situation. Lydia kept the house and raised Penny while I held a job."

"I know she loved knitting," I said. "Did she have any other hobbies?"

"Scrapbooking," Penny said. "She was always making those books... cutting things out of magazines, buying beads and lettering down at the craft store. She loved it."

"Could I see one?" I asked. "I've always been interested in it, but I've never taken it up."

Penny rose from her chair and went upstairs, then came back down a moment later. She set down a blue book in front of me. I opened it to find pictures I never expected.

Women dressed in power suits carrying briefcases, riding in the back of limousines, drinking champagne in elegant restaurants, standing in front of a room of men, obviously in charge.

It was not the scrapbook of a lifelong housewife. I had expected something to do with gardening or baking, and certainly, knitting, considering Lydia had been the one to put it together.

"Huh. I've never seen that one," Ted said, his brow furrowed.

"I found it last night while I was going through the others," Penny replied. "It was tucked away."

"Does it... symbolize something?" Ted asked. "These women... what they represent is a pretty far jump from our own lives in a small town."

"Maybe she'd developed a liking for expensive, new and shiny things," Penny said, her voice dripping with sarcasm as she rolled her eyes.

"Penny, please stop and mind your manners. What do think of all this?"

"It totally symbolized something," Penny said, casting an accusing glare at her father. "I think Mom wished she hadn't become a homemaker and had persued her career in finance. She went to college for it and earned her degree, but she never did anything with it."

As I watched the exchange between the two, I wondered if Lydia had given up her dreams and career for Ted.

"That's nonsense," Ted said, sitting back in his chair. "When we married, we agreed we wanted a traditional home, which is the best way to raise a child."

"Says who?" Penny asked.

"Says me," Ted replied, his voice firm and authoritative. He could sure go from the nice guy to the boss in a short time, especially for a mild-mannered accountant.

"Well, your word isn't the law, no matter what you think," Penny muttered as she pushed back her chair and left the room.

"I'm sorry about her," Ted said. "She's always been difficult, but ever since her mother died, it's gotten even worse. She needs to find a husband and begin her life."

Pursing my lips together, I held back from commenting. Penny was young and should be living, not looking for a husband, unless she really wanted one.

"My wife was a good woman," Ted said. "She kept a clean house and made decent meals. I'll miss her."

As I stared at the man, I came to realize Lydia

hadn't been in a happy marriage if her husband could only remember she kept a tidy house and was a decent cook. Didn't he have anything to say about the woman herself, or perhaps, even after so many years of marriage, he never bothered to get to know her? Had she become invisible—someone to pick up his socks and scrub the toilet?

Ted sighed and ran his hand over his face. "She was survived by us, of course, and she also has a sister living in Utah. She's coming for the funeral."

I scratched down the information on my notebook. "When are you having the service?"

"Next week. Let me get the details for you in case you want to print it."

He rose from the table and left the kitchen. I grabbed the scrapbook and flipped through the pages. I saw bright, vibrant women in charge of their lives, succeeding in their endeavors. I wanted to talk to Penny about it more. Had Lydia told Ted she was unhappy, that she'd wasted her life, then they'd argued and he'd hit her with the fireplace poker? A crime of passion?

It seemed reasonable to me. I heard his footsteps in the hall, and I quickly closed the book and set it back the way it had been.

"Here's the information," he said, handing me a

slip of paper. I read the neat and tidy writing and recognized the address as the Baptist church. "We'll be having the service there."

"Would you mind if I came?"

"Actually, yes, I would. We want to keep it family and close friends."

"I understand."

And I truly did. I wouldn't want a reporter at my family member's funeral.

"Unfortunately, our time is up, Tilly," he said, checking his watch. "I scheduled you for twenty minutes, and I need to hustle over to the funeral home in ten minutes."

I slipped the paper in my pocket and grabbed my bag. "Of course. Thank you for your time."

He walked me to the front door, and I felt his stare on me while I hurried down the walkway to my truck. I waved as I pulled away from the curb, and he went inside and shut the door.

On impulse, I parked a few houses down. If he'd been telling the truth about needing to visit the funeral home, he'd drive out the opposite direction and wouldn't see me.

I waited a couple of minutes, then a car exited his garage and headed the other way. When he rounded the corner and was out of sight, I flipped my truck around and parked across from his home.

Before I could really think things through, I rushed up to the house and pounded on the door. No one answered. Could Penny have gone with him? I really needed to talk to her without her father present, so I banged on the panel once again.

She flung it open and narrowed her gaze at me, obviously angry. "You're persistent."

"I wanted to talk to you."

"You already have. Now go away and write your article about my mother."

"Penny, I know I'm not getting the full version of your mother. I'm getting your father's view of her. Tell me yours."

Her anger slowly seeped away and after a moment, she stepped aside to allow me in. I glanced over my shoulder, hoping Ted wouldn't return, then followed her back into the kitchen. But then I remembered they had the fancy-pants doorbell, as Mrs. Marple had called it. I wasn't sure how it worked, but I had to assume Ted either knew I had arrived back at the house, or he could easily discover it.

"I have no idea who'd want to murder my mom,

except my dad," Penny said. "But he's got an alibi at work for when she was killed."

Well, I certainly hadn't expected Penny to accuse her father of murder. "Why do you think your dad might have killed her?"

Penny sighed and glanced around the kitchen, as if she searched for answers. "This past year, she changed a lot. I don't know why, or what sparked it, but she's been different. My whole life she's been the good little wife. Whatever my dad said, it was law."

"But yet, she went to college."

"She did. Her parents were very faith focused. They believed she should have gotten married right out of high school and started a family, but she insisted on going to college. She never did anything with the degree because her family wanted her to do what they believed was best: Get married, have children, be a good wife."

"And so she did."

"Yes. I grew up in a household where the man is in charge. He leads the family. No one argues with his decisions."

"How did you feel about that?"

"It was hard. I mean, when I was younger, I didn't realize the dynamics in our family were anything but normal. But as I got older, I saw my mom as a doormat, especially when I realized other women were running their own businesses, that they'd chosen not to be married, that they did things like travel the world by themselves. I lost a lot of respect for her until this past year."

"You don't know what changed her?"

Penny shook her head. "I honestly don't. But in these months, I've heard her argue with my father more than she'd ever done in the past. About a week before she died, he asked what was for dinner and she told him to cook his own. She wasn't the house chef and dishwasher."

"How did he take that?"

"He went through the roof. I thought he was going to hit her, but thankfully, he didn't."

"And you'd never seen her act that way before?"

"Never. She'd become defiant and mouthy toward my dad, and she encouraged me over and over to move out of the house and go live my life. She said she didn't want me to waste my days like she'd wasted hers."

What a perfect segue for me.

"I understand you moved to Los Angeles right after high school," I ventured.

"Yes. It was my attempt at trying to become a model."

"But you came back. Why?"

"Because I failed," Penny said with a shrug. "I was too short, too thin, not thin enough, too blonde, too pale, not blonde enough... I was never right for anything."

"So you came home to lick your wounds, so to speak," I said with a smile.

"Yes, I suppose so, and to try to figure out what to do with my life."

Of course, being five-foot-two, modeling had never been on my radar. I did know the industry could be brutal and unforgiving. "You're a beautiful girl, Penny. I hope you don't give up on your dreams if you still want to become a model."

Her cheeks flamed pink and she cast her gaze to the table. "Thank you. My dad is actually trying to get me to marry."

"How do you feel about that?"

"I don't want to be married," she said, sitting up straight in her chair, as if to assert her independence.

"Then don't," I said, rising to my feet. "You do what you want to do, Penny. If you don't want to get married, then get a job. Save your money. Get your own place."

She nodded as she opened the front door. "I do

have a job and I'm saving money. I can't wait to get out of here."

I turned to her and studied her once again. Was she on drugs? Probably not, but I thought I'd ask. If she wanted help, I'd tell Derek about her.

"Penny, the gossip vine tells me that you're a bit of a wild child," I said. "That you have a drug problem and sleep around."

She furrowed her brow. "Really? How strange. I don't do drugs."

With a grin, I waved goodbye and noted she didn't deny any bed hopping, which was fine. To each their own. Her father would have an absolute fit if he ever knew the truth.

Something had happened this past year that had made Lydia snap in a way. She had taken a hard look at her life and decided she wasn't happy about it, and she let her husband know. Ted Tillwacker didn't like it one bit.

As I drove away, I didn't think Penny killed her mother.

But her dad? That was another story.

10

FOR TWO DAYS I found it difficult to concentrate on anything but Lydia Tillwacker's murder. There were those who had motive, like her husband, who didn't like the woman she'd become, and Nancy Jones, who coveted the title of President of the Knitting Club. Then there was Mrs. Marple, who conveniently fit the police narrative. Was she strong enough to hit Lydia and kill her? I believed so, but I couldn't imagine her committing murder. She was still on my list of suspects simply because it sure as heck looked like she'd done it. However, I knew from experience that circumstantial evidence didn't equate to guilt.

My house looked great with the Christmas lights Derek had strung up. We also decorated a tree and I baked some cookies—sugar free, of course. Frank Sinatra and Dean Martin crooned classic Christmas tunes from my old stereo. The holiday spirit was alive and well in my home, and every time I looked over my land and saw Derek's empty house, I couldn't help but feel he should just move into mine. We already lived together, yet I appreciated that if things didn't work out, he had somewhere else to go on quick notice. But then, I also considered this sabotage on the relationship itself. Was I committed or not?

I sure had a tendency to frustrate myself with my constant roundabout of doubt, followed by self-correction.

Derek and I shared the couch on the lazy Sunday afternoon, watching Die Hard. Tinker snored softly at our feet and Belle snuggled up next to me. Meanwhile, we debated whether the movie was truly a Christmas movie, or if it was a movie that took place during Christmas. There was a big difference to me.

"Christmas movies are about the holiday spirit, about the feelings that come about this time of year," I argued.

"Wrong, Tilly," Derek said with a grin. "Die Hard is one of the best Christmas movies around."

"It's about him killing a bunch of terrorists. Just

because there's a decorated tree in it doesn't make it a holiday movie."

We lightheartedly disagreed for a few more moments, then finally settled that we were both right as my phone buzzed.

"There's supposed to be a big storm moving in tomorrow," I said, picking up the device. "I just got notification."

"Well, hopefully we won't get too much snow."

My phone rang while in my hand and startled me so badly, I threw it up in the air as if I were holding a snake. "Oh, no!" I yelled as it plunked to the carpet a few feet away from the sleeping Tinker. Belle jumped to her feet, arched her back and hissed at me, then ran out of the room.

"Sorry, Belly-Belle!" I called after her, knowing I wouldn't see her for a few hours. That cat held grudges better than any I'd ever met.

"I hope it isn't cracked," Derek said as I stood and retrieved it. "But then again, at least I could buy you a new one and I would have something to put under the tree for you."

"We agreed on no presents last night," I said, glancing at the screen. "You promised me."

"Yes, ma'am. No presents."

"Hey, Debbie," I answered while meandering

into the kitchen. I really didn't want to see Bruce Willis' bloody feet.

"Tilly!" she whispered. "I'm so glad you picked up!"

"What's wrong?" I asked, also lowering my voice.

"Nothing! I have more clues for you, super sleuth."

"Oh! Tell me! Because I have no idea who killed Lydia Tillwacker and I need all the help I can get!"

"Okay, listen up," Debbie murmured. "Mrs. Marple was just in here with two members of the knitting club. They've all left the group. Gone totally AWOL. I don't think it's going to survive."

"What does that have to do with Lydia's death?" I asked as I opened the refrigerator and stared inside. I wasn't hungry, but old habits die hard.

"Nothing. That's not the good part."

I shut the fridge and retrieved a glass of water. "Then what's the good part?"

"The three women were talking and I couldn't help but overhear that a couple of weeks ago, Lydia Tillwacker got someone in Little River fired. A clerk over at the dollar store."

I laughed, not because Lydia had caused someone to lose their job, but because Debbie had just happened to "overhear" the conversation. The image of her with a glass to her ear pressed against a wall came to mind. Debbie never "accidently" overheard anything but made it her business to eavesdrop if she wasn't included in the conversation.

"Tell me what happened," I said.

"Well, apparently, one of the women—I can't recall her name—was shopping with Lydia that day. The associate in the store was rude when Lydia asked a question about an expiration date on a product. He told her to take her fat butt outside and not come back. Lydia's friend said that normally Lydia would have burst out into tears and left, but instead, she stood up for herself and demanded to see a manager."

"That's an awful thing for the worker to say."

"I agree, and Lydia wasn't having any of it."

The scenario matched what Penny had indicated. Her quiet, subservient mother had changed dramatically and after years of allowing people to walk all over her, she'd asserted herself.

"What happened then?" I asked.

"Well, things got very heated, according to the story I overheard. The clerk yelled at her, but Lydia kept calm and demanded to see the manager. After a few moments, the manager finally showed up. Apparently, she'd been on her lunch break and smoking a cigarette outside. Not a nice habit, if you ask me."

"I feel the same," I replied. "Can we get back to the story though?"

"Sure. Anyway, Lydia explained what had happened and she demanded that the clerk be fired."

"That seems a little extreme to me," I said. "I mean, the clerk wasn't nice to say the least, but taking away someone's livelihood... that's taking things a little far."

"Taking things too far?" Debbie shrieked. "She may as well have shot for the dang moon!"

"Shh, Debbie!" I hissed. "Are they still sitting in your bakery? You were whispering when you called me, but now you're practically shouting!"

"You're right," Debbie said, her voice returning to a hushed tone. "I got carried away there. I just think what she did was very wrong."

I did as well, but I didn't understand what any of it had to do with Lydia's death. Sometimes, Debbie was able to see scenarios that I couldn't. "And this relates to Lydia's murder... how?"

"The woman who was with Lydia... she said that the clerk was absolutely furious about being fired. He said that he would make sure Lydia paid for what she'd done. The ladies were speculating that perhaps he'd followed through with the threat."

"Oh my," I muttered. "That is definitely something we need to consider in this whole mess."

"I thought so too," Debbie said. "If he was angry enough, he could have definitely done her in."

"Mrs. Marple told us that the Tillwackers have one of those fancy pants doorbells that sends a signal to a person's phone whenever there is movement," I said. "I would think that if that man showed up at the house, it would display on the recorded feed."

"Unless he went through the back door," Debbie said. "You brought up that possibility to the police when you went to the station."

"You're right," I said. Having told Debbie the whole sordid story of my interrogation, she was fully informed, and that included Byron's off the record talk about our relationship. "If I was going to hurt someone, I certainly wouldn't go through the front door. I'd be afraid a neighbor would see me."

"Same here."

I tried to imagine the scenario. Perhaps the clerk had watched her house for a few days and noted everyone's pattern of coming and going. Then he snuck around the side yard and came in through the back door.

"Do they have a gate that leads from the front yard to the back?" Debbie asked.

"Yes."

"What about the backyard fence? Do they have a gate leading out from their yard to beyond the house?"

"No. Their backyard fence butts up against their back neighbors."

"Well, then he'd have to creep along the side yard and go in through the side gate to get to the back door," Debbie said, mirroring my thoughts.

"Hmm... maybe you're right, but it would still be a bold move. He'd have to park on her street, walk down the sidewalk, then move between the two houses to get to her backyard. One of the neighbors would have had to see him. Wouldn't they?"

"You'd think so." The door chime in Debbie's store sounded in the background. "I've got to go. A customer just walked in."

"Is business getting better?" I asked.

"A little bit," she replied. "That nonsense about my donut killing Lydia needs to blow over, so get out there and find the killer, sneaky spy."

The line went dead and I set down my phone.

What the clerk had said had been very rude, but had it been worth raising such a ruckus about it that the manager fired him? Could a man get angry enough about losing his job to kill someone? Maybe I needed to question some of Lydia's neighbors and ask them whether they'd seen anyone sneaking around the area between the time Mrs. Marple left and I arrived. Or perhaps he'd lain in wait at the house earlier until Mrs. Marple was no longer there, then he struck.

For all I knew, he could have been headed out the back door as I entered the front. A chill ran over me at the thought. What if I'd come close to becoming his second victim and only missed him by minutes?

"What's up, Tilly?" Derek called from the living room. "The best line of the movie is right around the corner!"

"I'm coming," I said with a laugh. The movie was great and I did enjoy it—I just didn't believe anyone should refer to it as a Christmas movie.

"Who called?" he asked as I settled in next to him.

"Debbie. She had another theory on who killed Lydia Tillwacker."

"What is it?"

I explained it all to him, and he nodded. "It definitely should be explored. Just be careful, okay?"

"Of course."

Both of us startled when a knock sounded on the door. Tinker jumped to her feet and tore around the corner barking as if her tail end had caught fire.

I wondered who it could be, and decided not to answer. What if it was Byron? My stomach knotted at the thought. I didn't want to deal with him.

"Aren't you going to see who it is?" Derek asked.

"No."

"Why not?"

"I'm just happy sitting here with you," I said with a shrug. "And besides, I'm not expecting anyone. Whoever it is isn't welcome right now."

"Are you sure about that?"

I glanced out the window and didn't see a vehicle. "It's probably Minnie looking for her stupid cows. There isn't a car in the driveway."

The knock sounded again, and Derek stood. "I'll answer it for you."

As I watched him round the corner, I sighed. I should really answer my own door. The creak of the hinges filtered through the room, and I waited to hear voices to identify my unwanted visitor.

None came.

"Derek?" I called as I got to my feet. "Who is it?"

Rounding the corner, I gasped and immediately became lightheaded. I recognized the feeling from Derek's marriage proposal as my knees buckled and I thought I would pass out.

"Oh, my goodness!" I exclaimed.

11

———

"TILLY!" Mama said as she opened her arms and took me into a strong embrace. I stood stunned, glancing over her shoulder to see Hank grinning at us. His gray beard seemed thicker, but his gaze danced with happiness and good-natured mischief. My eyes stung and tears tracked down my cheeks while I wrapped my arms around my mom.

"What... How... Y-you said you couldn't come this year!" I exclaimed as she held me at arm's length and gave me the motherly once over.

Hank moved in and wrapped me in his arms, then deposited a quick kiss on top of my head. The man stood a few inches over six feet and right around two-fifty. It was like being swallowed up in love when he hugged me.

"We weren't going to come out," Hank said, his Louisiana accent thick. "But Derek here gave us a call and offered to fly us out."

"At first we said no," my mama said. "But this man can be very persuasive. He even got us an Uber from the airport! Technology these days is really amazing!"

"We were hoping we'd surprise you," Hank said. "So we waited for the driver to leave before knocking."

As I swiped at my tears, I glanced over at Derek. He leaned against the wall, holding on to Tinker's collar so she wouldn't jump on our new guests.

"I can't believe you did this," I said.

"Merry Christmas, Tilly," he replied with a shrug.

He let go of Tinker as I hugged him and gave him a quick kiss. I'd been firm on the fact that I didn't want any Christmas gifts under the tree, but I couldn't have imagined that he'd do something like pay for my parents to fly out. "Well, honey, these are my parents. Mama, Hank, this is Derek."

More embraces were given, accolades of appreciation were issued, and I finally got my wits about me. I no longer wanted to wilt to the floor.

"What's for dinner, Tilly?" Hank asked. "I'm starving!"

"I'll take the suitcases to their room," Derek said, grabbing one in each hand.

"Just a minute, son," Hank said. "I've got to get something out of there." Derek set down the bag, and my stepdad rummaged through the front pocket, then retrieved a flask. "Y'all can take that up there for us now. Thank you."

As he ascended the stairs, Mama leaned in and whispered, "Oh, he's a cute one, Tilly."

"Nice catch," Hank agreed. "If I were you, I'd keep that one around. Don't throw him back."

"Thank you," I replied. "I do like him. Come into the kitchen. I can make some tea and I'll get dinner figured out."

As they followed me, I cringed when I thought about their bedroom. Housekeeping wasn't one of my strong suits, and that layer of dust I'd seen in there the other day hadn't wiped up itself.

"Tell us what you've been up to, girl," Hank said as he sat down at the kitchen table. "You still hunting a killer?"

"I am," I replied, pulling down my pitcher from the cabinet.

"That's my girl," Hank said, his voice full of pride.

"Tilly, you need to be careful!" Mama exclaimed. "It's so dangerous!"

"Your mom is right on that one," Hank said with a nod as he poured a little liquid from his flask into the tea I served him. "Gators are more personable than most humans these days."

Derek thumped down the stairs to join us, and after a minute, we all sat at the table. I studied my parents carefully since I hadn't seen them in three years.

My mom had aged a bit, and she definitely now looked like she sat firmly in her sixties. Her husband still reminded me of Santa Claus, but I noted more lines around his eyes.

"Who do you think did it?" Hank asked.

"I'm not sure yet," I replied. "As usual, there are a lot of suspects."

"Tell us about it, honey," Mama said, reaching across the table and squeezing my hand.

As I went over the changes people had noticed in Lydia as well as the list of potential killers—Lydia's husband, Mrs. Marple, Nancy Jones and the unnamed clerk at the dollar store in Little River— they both listened intently.

"It's the husband," Hank declared. "Definitely the husband."

"Why do you say that?" Derek asked.

Hank sipped some more of his tea as he put his thoughts together. "Now, I'm going to preface this by saying this has nothing to do with your mama, Tilly. She is the best thing that ever came into my life, and I think she's darn perfect with her good-natured, sassy ways. Her teasing and the fact she's such a strong lady are what attracted me to her, understand?"

I had never really seen that side of my mom until she met Hank. He brought out some deep happiness that had been buried within her. She loved to laugh, and sassy was a good description.

I glanced over at her and nodded. "Okay."

"Aww... you're such a big oaf," Mama said, playfully slapping Hank's shoulder. "Tell me more."

"Later, love," Hank said with a wink. "I don't want to lose my train of thought."

"Oh, no. We don't want that," she replied. "Please, go on."

He cleared his throat and his brow furrowed in seriousness. "When a man and a woman get married, they aren't the same people ten years later, or even five years later. People change. A lot of times, they can change together in harmony. They can still cling to that core thing that brought them together in the first place. For me, it was your mom's good heart, her smile, and that loud, snorty laugh she has.

"But sometimes, when people change it causes discord, which is the case in the Tillwacker marriage. Mrs. Tillwacker went from a person who allowed everyone to walk all over her to an assertive woman who wanted to take control of her life. I promise you, her husband didn't like that one bit."

"They were very religious," I said. "I've been told that they believed the man is the head of the household. His rule is law. Until recently, that's the way it was, then Lydia changed and started standing up for herself not only at home, but other places as well."

"And didn't you say there were rumors he was having an affair?" Derek asked.

"Yes," I replied with a nod.

"Bingo!" Hank exclaimed. "There you have it. Case closed. Wife finds out he's having an affair and calls him out on it. He gets mad at her for raising her voice, so there you have your killer."

"A crime of passion, honey?" my mom asked.

"Passionate rage," Hank replied. "I've seen men throw their wives to the gators for less."

Mama giggled as Derek's eyes widened. Hank

glanced over at him and burst out laughing. "Just kidding, son. I've heard stories, but I've never seen it."

Derek grinned and his shoulders sagged while he squeezed my hand under the table. "I'm glad to hear that."

Hank sounded crazy sometimes, and he also had loads of good stories. Whether they were true or not, nobody was ever sure.

We chatted about dinner and decided on hamburgers, corn on the cob, and a salad. Mama and I worked in the kitchen while sipping on some wine and Hank insisted Derek give him a tour of the house and property. Personally, I thought I may burst with happiness and tears welled once again. Christmas was going to be perfect.

THE STORM never brought any snow, but the temperature plummeted into the twenties, making the next morning so cold, I didn't want to emerge from my comforter.

Once I was up and around, Mama asked me to take her into town to do a little shopping. Since I had to work, she and Derek decided he'd pick her up in front of my office at noon. I introduced her to Harold, then we went over to Debbie's Deliciousness so my mom could meet her and Carla.

When I'd married Tommy, I really didn't have any friends of my own. The ceremony had consisted of my parents and some of Tommy's buddies from high school and their wives. It wasn't until after Tommy left me that I developed real relationships.

Debbie's place was a little busier, but not much. The bakery had once been a hub of activity in the morning, but I counted six other customers besides us. Debbie's face lit up when she saw us and she stuck her head in the back. Carla emerged seconds later, and they both rounded the counter with huge grins.

"This is your mom!" Debbie exclaimed with certainty as she took Mama into an embrace. "I can see the resemblance."

"You said she wasn't coming for Christmas!" Carla said, lining up for a hug.

"Mama, these are my two best friends," I said. "That's Debbie, and this is Carla."

"It's so nice to meet you two!" my mom said. "I'm assuming this is your store, Debbie?"

"Yes, it is. Carla here helps me manage it. Best partner I could ever have."

"That's wonderful," Mama said, glancing around. "This is such a warm, homey place. It's smells delicious. Is that nutmeg? Maybe some cinnamon?"

"Yes, it is. Let's sit you down and you can sample the goods!" Carla said, linking arms with my mom and guiding her to our favorite table tucked in the corner.

Debbie rushed back around the display counter and emerged a few moments later with a tray of assorted goodies. She set them on the table, then rushed back for coffees.

"These look amazing," Mama crooned.

"The ones with the pink flags are sugar free," Carla said. "They're really popular."

"Those are what I like," I said, grabbing a strawberry filled donut.

"We're trying to figure out how we can sell them beyond the store," Carla said. "I'm working out the details."

"I want confectionary world dominance," Debbie stated, setting down our drinks. "And also sugar-free supremacy."

"Let's start with Northern California first," Carla said, rolling her eyes. "Then we can branch out slowly until you rule the donut world."

"Well, I think you ladies will achieve that," my

mom said with a groan as she took a second bite. "Debbie, these taste like angels made them and dropped them directly from heaven."

"Well, thank you," my friend said softly. "I really appreciate that."

Mama asked a ton of questions about their lives and both were open books. Carla told her all about her marriage to Mac, their fabulous honeymoon cruise they'd taken earlier in the year, and she surprised even me when she said they were going to try to have some kids.

"I thought Francis was your baby," I said.

"Francis is a cat," Carla replied. "He's a cranky baby, but I think I'm ready for the real deal."

I'd never get pregnant due to medical issues, and I was okay with that. Happiness for my friend surged through me, and I also got a little excited. "Can I babysit?"

"Of course," Carla said, giggling. "But don't get too ahead of yourself, Tilly. There needs to be a baby first."

"No babies, no man for me," Debbie said. "I'm married to these four walls and I'm really happy about that."

"And that's okay, too!" Mama said. "Every woman

has to find her way and what's going to make her happy."

As the discussion continued, my thoughts once again returned to Lydia Tillwacker's death. What had been the catalyst for her extreme change this past year? She seemed to have a lot of regrets, if what Penny said had been true. Had Hank been right in his theory that Ted Tillwacker just couldn't take the outspoken woman who stood up for herself any longer? Or had Lydia died because she'd taken things too far and caused someone to lose their job? Had Nazi Nancy, as I'd grown to call her, wanted to head the knitting club so badly and execute her own plan for world domination, she'd offed Lydia? People had been killed for less.

My phone rang and I retrieved it from my pocket. I stood and went to the other side of the bakery.

"Hey, Harold. What's up?"

"You got a phone call on the office line a few minutes ago. A woman named Dorothy Bennett who says she wants to talk to you about the Tillwacker murder."

"Who is she?" I asked.

"She lives across the street from the Tillwackers and says she may have information on who killed Lydia."

12

———

I RETURNED Dorothy's phone call and she asked me to come to her home. Apparently, she suffered from agoraphobia and had a hard time leaving her house. She'd piqued my curiosity, so I didn't mind leaving Mama with Debbie and Carla. I could hear them all laughing even after I was out on the sidewalk and the bakery door had closed. Mama hadn't seemed to care, either.

When I arrived at Dorothy's, I decided to park down the street a ways—right across from Myra's home—just so my truck wasn't completely obvious to the Tillwackers. I hurried up the sidewalk to the front door and rang the bell.

A woman about my height with a brown bob,

dressed in a blue sweater and jeans, answered. I figured her to be in her sixties.

"Tilly?" she asked, glancing over my shoulder with worry.

"Yes."

"Come in, come in. Oh, it's so cold out there. You'll get frostbite if you're out too long."

A bit of an exaggeration, but I agreed. Winter had arrived in full force.

I followed her into the tidy living room furnished in browns and white. Natural light filled the space, filtering through the large picture window. A photo of a much younger Dorothy, and I assumed her family, sat on the fireplace mantle. I studied it for a moment before sitting down.

"That's my husband, Don, who died last year, and my kids, who now have their own families," she said. "They'll be coming to visit a couple of days before Christmas."

"Sounds like you'll have a houseful," I said, taking a seat on the couch. "That'll be nice for you."

"It will. I get lonely not being able to go out, but Debbie from the bakery stops by a couple of times a week with some groceries and donuts. She's a nice woman."

"I didn't know that," I replied, truly surprised. "Debbie's one of my good friends."

"Really? Oh, yes. She's a doll. I don't know where I'd be without her. She and my daughter, Susan, were great friends growing up and we've kept in touch over the years, even after Susan left for college. When Don died, Debbie took it upon herself to help me out."

Debbie sometimes acted tough, but she did have a heart of gold mushier than a bad avocado.

"So, what did you want to tell me?" I asked.

"First, thank you for coming to see me. I suppose I could have spoken to you over the phone, but I'll admit, my actions are selfish. I wanted company."

"That's okay," I replied. Mama was in great hands and said she had shopping to do while I worked. If Dorothy could give me information about Lydia's death and I could curb some of her loneliness for a little while, then I considered the visit a big win, not an inconvenience. "I'm happy to be here."

"Thank you for your understanding," Dorothy replied. "I told Debbie about this yesterday, and she suggested that I call you. She gave me your office number. I wasn't sure whether I wanted to disclose what I saw or not, so I waited until today to phone you."

"I realize getting involved can be scary."

"Yes," she said, looking out the window over my shoulder. "As I explained, I have severe agoraphobia. Just the thought of going down to the mailbox makes my heart skip and I begin to sweat. Because of this, I spend a lot of time looking out my window. It's not that I'm interested in other people's business, but I don't have anything else to do. There's nothing but garbage on the television anymore, and I enjoy reading, but that tends to get a little old as well. I have real life right outside my window, but I can only observe it."

For me, being at home was a treat—a time to relax, recharge, and spend time with the ones I loved. But the thought of being trapped in my home by some unseen, powerful force... I imagined Dorothy fought some level of depression on a daily basis.

She twisted her hands in her lap, her gaze still focused on the outside world. "Lydia was a nice woman. After Don died, she checked up on me a few times a month, bringing me a casserole or pie during her visits. She ran errands for me every now and then. I liked her and appreciated all her help. When I found out that she'd been murdered, I was crushed. I started to think about the things I've seen going on in the neighborhood and one episode stood out to me as particularly strange."

"What was that?"

"I guess it was a week or so before Lydia's death. I saw a man walking down the street. I didn't recognize him. He went right up the Tillwackers' walkway and knocked on the door a few times. He glanced around, as if searching for someone watching him. Then, he pulled out something from his jacket and put it on the door. Some type of Jimmy or something."

"So he tried to break in?"

Dorothy nodded. "That's certainly what it looked like. I saw the glint of metal in the sunlight."

"What happened then?"

"I called Ted Tillwacker, but he didn't answer. Then I called the sheriff and they said they'd send someone out. I kept my eye on him the whole time. I wanted to yell at him but I was afraid. What if he came after me?"

"That's perfectly understandable," I said. "You needed to keep yourself safe."

"It was so strange, Tilly... the intruder tried to jimmy the lock and suddenly, he stopped. Then he left the way he'd come."

"Interesting."

"I often wondered what happened. He was obviously trying to break in, but then he just stopped. Why?"

While I debated whether to tell her about the doorbell, I glanced over at the Tillwacker house. I didn't know how much of the neighborhood the camera would catch or if it only recorded what was taking place directly in front of the house.

"The Tillwackers have one of those doorbells that is motion activated," I said, once again facing Dorothy. "Once it's turned on, it records whoever is standing in front of it."

"I didn't know that!" Dorothy said, her eyes wide. "I've never heard of such a thing!"

"Yes, it's an interesting security tool," I replied. "Anyway, the doorbell probably notified Ted Tillwacker's phone and then he could have spoken to the burglar and told him to get lost."

Dorothy stared out the window for a long moment, then said, "You know, that's what it seemed like—his movements indicated he'd been caught now you've explained the doorbell to me. I bet you're right. The man scampered like a rabbit being chased by a mama grizzly."

"Have you told the sheriff about this?" I asked. "Did he come and take your statement?"

"It wasn't actually him, but one of his deputies. However, I didn't really feel as though he was listening to me. I'm the crazy woman who can't step out her front door without a panic attack. He didn't take me seriously."

"Was his name Byron?"

"No. It was something else. I have his card if you want it."

"That's okay," I replied quickly as she began to rise to her feet. "I don't need it."

Relief swept through me that it hadn't been Byron to take her statement. I didn't consider him that smart, but he was kind most of the time, and it sounded as if whoever had been here had blown off Dorothy as crazy.

She may not be able to go out of her home, but she definitely wasn't insane.

"I thought about this for days," she continued. "Then I saw the sheriff's cars and ambulance pull up in front of the house. A woman came out..." Her voice trailed off as she narrowed her gaze on me. "Was that you?"

"Yes. I found Lydia."

"Oh, my word!" she said, bringing her hand to her chest. "I had no idea! Debbie didn't tell me that!"

"I was standing out on the stoop while the police investigated," I said.

"You looked like you were about to freeze to death."

"It was definitely cold."

Dorothy shook her head. "The sheriff should have allowed you to stay inside. That was cruel."

"It was actually my choice," I replied. "I felt it was the best course of action." I didn't bother to mention that the sheriff and Byron had been complete turds to me that day.

"Well, then, I supposed it was okay if you chose to be out there," Dorothy murmured. She stared at the Tillwacker house for another long moment before speaking. "I was thinking about everything that happened prior to that awful day, and one thought keeps coming to me: what if that burglar came back and Lydia had been home? He'd know about that fancy doorbell, so he wouldn't go in the front door. But what if he went around the house to the back door?

Her theory sounded suspiciously identical to the idea Debbie had concocted about the clerk Lydia had gotten fired. Could we be talking about the same person? Were the clerk and the robber one and the same?

"Did you recognize the man at all when he was trying to break in?" I asked.

Dorothy shook her head. "No, but I didn't know it was you standing on that stoop either. Lydia used to complain that Ted never shoveled them and it drove her crazy. I saw you take that tumble. That looked painful."

"Yes, it was. Do you think she mentioned it to him?" I asked. I had a feeling this new Lydia that had emerged had given Ted an earful.

"I don't know. She did shovel them herself a couple of times. One morning I saw her yelling at him as he left for work while she cleared the snow, so perhaps she did. I couldn't hear what she said, though."

Another example of a woman at her wits' end. The more I considered it all, the more I felt Hank was right. Ted was the murderer. His wife going from a docile, subservient woman to one that regretted her life and would no longer keep her mouth shut had driven him over the edge.

As I tried to think of a way to identify if the burglar and the fired clerk were the same person, I decided to head over to the source and hope that Penny would answer the door and not Ted. I didn't think she would have any issues with me looking at their doorbell recordings.

"Was there something else, Dorothy?" I asked. "Can you think of anything that would help find Lydia's murderer?"

She shook her head. "When I mentioned the intruder to Debbie, she asked me to call you, especially since I'd already phoned the sheriff and received a lukewarm response. I just thought someone should know."

"I think you did the right thing," I said. "Technically, I report for the paper and I'm not out looking for the killer." It was a lie, but I didn't want word getting back to Byron or the sheriff that I intended to solve the case. "But that doesn't mean I'm not actively investigating it on a journalistic level."

"Of course," Dorothy said, getting to her feet. "I understand and appreciate you stopping by."

She walked me to the door and opened it. I hesitated before leaving when I saw Myra walking down the street toward the Tillwackers dressed in a parka and knee-high black boots and carrying a glass dish wrapped in foil.

"That's Myra," Dorothy said. "We used to be in the knitting club together. She's a good neighbor and has been bringing food to Ted and Penny since Lydia's death."

"How nice of her," I murmured. "She was so upset about losing her friend."

"I don't know if they were very friendly before Lydia died," Dorothy said. "Lydia told me they'd had a falling out."

"That's too bad. Did she say what it was about? Maybe the knitting club?"

"She did say that was part of it, but she didn't give me any details."

Myra knocked on the Tillwackers' door and Ted answered, then they both disappeared inside.

So much for my plan of visiting Penny.

"If you think of anything else, give me a call, okay?" I said as I pulled out my notepad and jotted down my phone number. "This is my personal cell phone."

Dorothy glanced at it and nodded. "You know, I hate that Lydia's gone. I did like her very much, but this is also so very exciting and scary for me. What if the information I've provided to the police helps them catch a killer? And what if the murderer somehow finds out that I'm involved? I feel like a sitting duck over here."

"You're going to be fine," I said with a grin. "Just

make sure to keep your house locked up and don't let strangers in."

"I won't," she said, opening the door for me. "You stay safe out there, Tilly. The world is a terribly dangerous place."

Especially when one hunted a murderer.

13

____

"Hi, honey!" Mama yelled from the kitchen when I arrived home in the late afternoon.

"Something smells good," I called as I slipped off my coat, hung it on the peg, and walked into the kitchen.

"I've got pot roast cooking," she said, hugging me. "Hank's been very busy here today—I just wanted to let you know."

While driving in, I had noted my back fence had a fresh coat of paint and the dead grass had been razed down to a tight half-inch.

"Derek's upstairs," she said. "I think Hank wore him out."

Belle sat on her corner of the countertop and I whispered hello and stroked her head. She eyed my mother warily and didn't seem too happy with our visitors.

"That cat won't move," Mama said. "I tried to shoo her a couple of times, but she's not having any of it."

"I know," I replied with a sigh. "She won the countertop battle and never lets anyone forget it. I'm going to go change."

As I trudged up the stairs, I noted the banister had been oiled and looked shiny and new, and I found Derek sprawled across the bed in our room.

"Everything go okay today?" I asked, giving him a quick kiss.

"I've been trying to keep up with Hank," Derek said with a yawn. "I thought old people were supposed to sit around and watch soap operas all day. Instead, he wanted to paint the fence and mow the lawn. He said it would grow back thicker than his beard in the summer if we took it down really low."

"He likes to have stuff to do," I said with a giggle as I changed into my sweatpants and sweatshirt.

"Well, he says that if the snow stays away, he's going to paint the shutters and clean the fireplace flue and the gutters. And he wants me to help."

"I'm sorry," I said, sitting down on the mattress. "He has a hard time sitting still for very long."

"It's fine," Derek replied, squeezing my hand. "I just can't believe his energy level. He's making me feel old."

I laughed again as I stood and tried to pull him up off the bed.

"He also tried to kill one of the chickens for dinner today," Derek said. "He was in the coop chasing them when I stopped him."

"Oh, no," I muttered. "I need to go have a talk with him. Tinker would be destroyed if we ate one of her hens."

"You go talk to him," Derek said, rolling over. "I just need to sleep for a little while."

As I bounded down the stairs, I wondered how Derek would make it through the next couple of weeks. My parents had always been super high energy and being around them could be absolutely exhausting. At least I got to escape them for a few hours by going to work.

I found Hank out in the garage rearranging the boxes and bins on the shelves. It needed to be done, so I appreciated his efforts.

"Hey, girl!" he said as he lifted a tub of old sheets

to the top shelf. "Just trying to organize your stuff here."

Why I bothered to keep the old sheets, I had no idea.

"Thanks. I appreciate your help and your painting and for cutting the lawn. But I need you to stay away from the chickens."

"Derek told me we couldn't eat them," Hank said, turning to me. "Something about them being Tinker's friends?"

I pulled open the door that led to the backyard area. Tinker lay by the coop, her nose stuck through the wiring. The chickens perched on each side of her snout. "See? Come look at this."

"Well, I'll be darned," Hank whispered. "Do you think she wants a piece of them?"

"I don't. I think she's in love with them, and I don't want to upset her by eating one."

Hank laid his hand on my shoulder and laughed. "I understand. I'll drop the idea."

"How's Irwin?" I asked, shutting the door.

"Oh, he's great. He was gone a long time during mating season, so I'm sure the swamp is filled with lots of his offspring. He's a good boy."

To others, it probably sounded funny listening to Hank describe a six-foot gator as a 'good boy,' but it was just life to me. Everyone had a quirky thing that made them unique and different.

"You don't have to do all this," I said, motioning to the shelves. "Derek and I will get it done once we have time."

"It's not a bother, Tilly," Hank said with a grin. "Just between you and me, I'm afraid if I stop moving, the Grim Reaper will catch me. If it's okay, I'll just keep tinkering around."

"That's fine," I said, heading back into the house. "Knock yourself out!"

I'd heard him say the same thing before. The first time, I thought he had been telling me he was going to die and I'd panicked. But then he assured me that he'd be keeping Death at bay for a long time and asked me not to worry about such things.

I returned to the kitchen and helped Mama get the salad ready.

"Your friends are lovely," she said. "We had such a good time this morning."

"Did you get your shopping done?" I asked, slicing a tomato.

"Yes, and then I met Derek and he brought me back here. "He's sure a sweetie, Tilly, and he loves you very much."

"I know," I said with a sigh. "We're living

together, but he still has his house. We should get married, but I did throw up all over him last time he asked."

Mama laughed and shook her head. "That was unfortunate. I'm just glad you didn't get a concussion when you hit the floor."

"Me, too. Derek was there with me in the hospital as well."

"Do you want to marry him, Tilly?"

"Some days, yes," I replied with a sigh. "Other days, my insecurities come back to haunt me. What if my relationship with him crashes like my marriage to Tommy did?"

My mom came over and laid her hand on my forearm. "And what if it doesn't?"

I turned and met her gaze. She stared at me with so much love and wisdom, I couldn't help but hang on to every word.

"Sometimes, you have to take chances, Tilly. You have to trust others. I can tell you right now Derek is much different from Tommy. Much different. He's a good man with a good heart. If you feel ready to get married on more days than you don't, then do it. Or, if you're happy with the way things are, then keep them that way. Just be happy. That's all any mother wants for her children."

She made it all sound so simple. Maybe it was and I stood too close to it all to see it for what it really was: my own anxieties blocking my view.

An hour later, we sat around the table eating Mama's delicious pot roast. Tinker stared up at me with her big brown eyes, trying to convince me she hadn't eaten in weeks and if she didn't get a piece of meat right then, she may die.

"Give it up, girl," I muttered. "You just ate ten minutes ago. You aren't fooling anyone."

"So did you catch your killer today, Tilly?" Hank asked, dumping some liquor from his flask into his diet cola.

"Unfortunately, no."

"The husband did it," Hank said. "Mark my words."

"Well, if you're right, I need proof."

"You'll find it," Hank said reassuringly. "I have faith in my girl."

The knock at the door startled me and I exchanged glances with Derek. He furrowed his brow in confusion.

"I'll get it," I said, standing and walking to the front door. Byron stood on my porch dressed in full sheriff uniform—including a star on his lapel I'd never noticed and a big parka—and I groaned inwardly, because I was too polite to actually voice my dismay.

"Hey, Tilly!" he said loudly. "I heard your parents were in town and thought I'd stop by and meet them!"

"Well, we're eating," I said softly. "It's really not a good time."

"Oh, it's fine, honey," my mom said from behind me. "We've got plenty of food for your friend."

Byron pushed his way past me and introduced himself to my mom, asking how her trip was, if she liked Oak Peak... while calling her ma'am at least a half-dozen times.

Hank rounded the corner. "It's always a pleasure to meet an officer of the law! Come in, son, come in!"

Byron shook hands with Hank and I trailed into the kitchen behind them. Derek and I stared at each other for a moment, then he shook his head as if he couldn't believe Byron's boldness either.

Derek stood and shook the deputy's hand while my mom got him a plate. We all sat down and I glared daggers at Byron, who studiously ignored me and concentrated solely on my parents.

All smiles, laughter and chit-chat, I didn't understand what he was trying to achieve with this visit, but whatever it was, I didn't like it in the least bit.

The conversation became a three-way event between Hank, Byron, and my mom. Derek and I suddenly found ourselves on the outs.

"Are you looking for that killer that's on the loose?" Hank asked.

"We certainly are, sir," Byron said. "We've got some great leads and we'll be making an arrest soon."

His gaze slid over to Derek and held there for a brief moment, then moved back to Hank.

"Tilly's searching for the murderer as well," Hank said. "Just so you know, it's the husband. He did it."

"No, I'm not trying to find the killer," I replied with a smile. "I'm a reporter who is looking into the case. I'm certainly not trying to solve it."

A lie, but the last thing I needed from Byron was a lecture on how I needed to allow the police to do their jobs when I had every intention of solving the case before their office did.

"Well, that's not very smart," Byron said. "But then again, Tilly does sometimes make poor choices."

I set down my fork, fighting the urgency to stab him with it as my anger seethed. First, he came barging into my home without an invitation, and now, he wanted to discuss what he considered my poor choices with people he just met?

I had an idea of where the conversation was headed because we'd been here before. "What does that mean?" I asked through a clenched jaw.

Byron's stare remained focused on my parents. "It means that instead of dating a man who has promised to uphold the law, you've decided to date a drug addict, a man who's spent more years than not breaking laws."

Mama gasped and Hank stared wide-eyed.

"Get out!" I yelled as I shot to my feet. "Who I date is my business and not yours! And for the record, I wouldn't go out with you if you were the last man on this Earth!"

A heavy silence settled over the room as Byron snickered, then shook his head as if I were the one out of line.

"Get out!" I screamed again.

"You heard her," Derek said quietly. "She asked you leave and I think it would be a good idea if you didn't come back."

Byron stared Derek down for a long moment, his fist clenched around his fork. Finally, he stood, and I was afraid they'd come to blows as he walked out of the kitchen. When he finally left, the door sounded like a shotgun going off in the quiet.

"Excuse me," Derek murmured and headed up the stairs.

"We didn't know that about Derek," Hank said softly. "Did you, Tilly?"

I nodded as I sat down. "Yes. He's been very open and honest with me about his past. He's been sober ten years, going on eleven."

"Oh, my," Mama murmured.

"I believe people can change," I continued. "I know I'm not the same person I was six months ago, let alone two years ago."

Hank nodded and sipped his tea. "I agree, honey. That wasn't nice of Byron to come busting in here like that and reveal things that aren't his business. That boy should be ashamed of himself."

"We didn't know, Tilly," Mama said, reaching across the table to grab my hand. "We thought he was your friend and wanted to make him feel welcome."

"I know, Mama. I dated Byron very briefly, and he's been after me ever since. He's also been horrible to Derek."

"He sure puts on a good game face," Hank said. "I never would have guessed he's a turd in disguise."

"I'm going to head upstairs and talk to Derek," I said, rising from the table.

"Let me do it," Hank replied. "He needs to hear it from the horses' mouth that we don't think anything less of him."

Tears welled in my eyes as Hank meandered up the stairs.

Mama squeezed my hand. "You're happy, Tilly. The happiest I've seen you in a long time. That's all that matters to us."

Mama and I sat in silence while the male voices wafted down the stairs.

"Let's get this cleaned up," she said, staring at the half-filled plates. "I know I've lost my appetite."

"Me, too," I replied.

"I'll make a couple of extra plates in case Hank and Derek want some later."

As we did the dishes, I couldn't think of anything but Byron. What had gotten into him? It didn't surprise me that he knew my parents were in town, but his actions definitely did. It was almost as if he'd lost his mind.

I began to wonder if *he* was the one on drugs.

14

DEREK and I stayed up late into the night discussing Byron. Well, he railed on about what a no-good jerk Byron was, and I listened.

"I'm not ashamed of my past," Derek said through gritted teeth. "But he had no business coming in here and announcing it to your parents like that."

"No, he didn't."

"He's trying to break us up, Tilly," Derek growled. "He's trying to turn your parents against me."

I laid my hand on his forearm. "Derek, it doesn't matter what my parents think. I love you and I'm happy. I know your heart is good and that your past doesn't define who you are now. We grow and change every single day. I'm not the same person I was even six months ago."

He sighed and ran his hand through his hair. "I love you, too. Byron was so out of line, Tilly, I want to lodge my fist in between his teeth."

Frankly, so did I, but I had other ideas on how to land the proverbial punch, and number one on my list was solving the Lydia Tillwacker murder.

The next morning, I woke to the sound of Hank, Mama, and Derek laughing downstairs. The drama from the previous night seemed to have passed. My parents weren't ones to judge another, and I would be forever grateful for that. I wanted them to like Derek and vice versa.

Byron's antics the previous night had only fueled my desire to solve Lydia's murder. Beforehand, I had wanted to find the killer, but it had almost become a joke between me and my friends—Tilly trumps the sheriff's office once again. Now, however, I wanted to make them look like fools and rub my superior sleuthing skills right in Byron's arrogant face.

As I showered and dressed, I planned out my day. My first stop would be the Tillwacker house so I could talk to Penny alone. But first, I had to make sure Ted wasn't home.

Derek met me at the bottom of the stairs with a

quick kiss and handed me a cup of coffee with a dollop of cream. Just the way I liked it. Mama and Hank each gave me a hug as if they wanted me to know they were behind me and my choice in men one hundred percent.

"What's on the agenda today while I'm at work?" I asked.

"I'm taking Hank over to the old Rupert house," Derek said. "There are some things there that need fixing and he said he'd love to help out."

"Does that mean you're going to sell it?" I asked.

"I don't know," Derek said. "It's a perfectly good house with an amazing plot of land, and it seems like a waste to just have it sit there."

Derek still hadn't done anything besides raze the nectarine orchard. The house stood empty, and he vacillated between selling It or not. Neither of us had any desire for any more cows in our small neighborhood—Minnie's were plenty. He also wanted to make sure we both liked whoever purchased the house. All Derek had to do was buy the land our other neighbor, Minnie, lived on, and he'd own everything his father had originally sold that had made Derek so wealthy.

But we both knew Minnie wasn't going anywhere.

"Whatever you decide to do is great with me," I said. "Like we agreed, just no more cows."

"No. Absolutely not."

The scent of cow poo could be pretty powerful, especially during the hot, summer months.

After saying my goodbyes and stepping out into the bitter cold, I entered my truck and headed to work, once again thankful the snow had stayed at bay. Secretly, I hoped for a white Christmas, but I wouldn't tell Debbie. It would ruin my history of complaining about the snow, which drove Debbie crazy, and I kind of relished in that just a little bit.

The long drive into town also gave me an amazing idea.

"Good morning, Tilly!" Harold boomed as I walked in. "Anything new and exciting?"

"No," I said. Harold didn't need to hear about my family drama. "Not a thing."

"Can you write a piece on the Christmas bouquets available at the florist?" Harold asked. "And how are we looking with other stories on the Tillwacker murder?"

"Well, I was actually wondering if you could get me an appointment to talk to Doctor Wheeler. I have some questions for him."

Boom. My amazing idea was now out in the open.

Harold arched an eyebrow at me as he stared over his glasses. "I can do that, but I don't think we can print anything he says because it's a police investigation."

"I know, Harold," I said with a smile. "I just have a few questions about the murder that I wanted to clear up for myself."

"I'll give him a call. How's your schedule tomorrow?"

"Wide open. The afternoon would be best."

As he picked up his phone, I dumped my bag on my desk and turned on my computer. I typed in Ted Tillwacker's name and Oak Peak and quickly found his work number. After pressing the digits on my own phone that would hide my identity to his office, I called.

"Reedy and Associates," the reception said, her voice crisp and clear.

"Is Ted Tillwacker in today?" I asked. "I have a certified delivery that he needs to sign for."

"I can sign for it," she said.

Dang it. I was hoping she'd just give me his schedule. "Well, my boss said that Mr. Tillwacker needs to sign. It's my first week on the job and I don't want to get in trouble. If I could get his schedule for the day, that would be great."

The receptionist sighed and I heard the tapping of a computer. "He'll be in at nine today and has checked himself out from twelve to one, then he's back in the office again until four."

"Thank you," I said, glancing at the clock. "I appreciate your help."

If I left now, Ted would be arriving at work by the time I got to his house.

"Gotta go!" I called over my shoulder, stuffing my phone in my bag and I ran out of the office to my truck.

It bothered me how easily the lie to the receptionist had come, but I would do just about anything to solve Lydia's murder before the sheriff's office.

I hurried over to the Tillwacker street and pulled in a few houses down, just past Myra's. Ted's car was still in the driveway, so apparently, he was running a little late.

After a few minutes of staring in the rearview mirror, Myra walked down the street coming from the direction of the Tillwacker's, then entered her own home.

"Early morning visit," I mumbled as I picked up my phone and dialed Debbie.

"What's up, Tilly?"

"Is Ted Tillwacker having an affair or not?"

"That's the rumor, but I don't know with who."

"Hmm… is Myra Kent married?"

"No. Her husband left. I don't know much about it."

Ted's car pulled out into the street and headed off the other way. "Okay, I have to go."

If I could prove that Ted and Myra were an item, maybe I could solidify my suspicions that Ted was the murderer and killed Lydia to get her out of the way so he could continue his sordid affair.

It would have to wait. I had another fish to fry.

After exiting my car, I hurried down the sidewalk. Penny answered my knock right away.

"What's up?" she asked, tossing her ponytail behind her.

"I was wondering if you had access to everything your doorbell catches," I asked, looking over my shoulder. I felt a stare on me from across the street and fought the urge to wave at Dorothy.

"It's in the storage cloud. I can access it."

"Great! Can I see it?"

She narrowed her gaze at me. "Why? What's going on?"

"One of your neighbors told me she saw

someone approach your home between the time Mrs. Marple left and I arrived. I was hoping to see who it was."

"Sure," Penny replied, stepping aside. "The cops have already looked at it, but I don't see a problem with you doing the same."

I followed her into the kitchen and she flipped open a laptop on the kitchen counter. "Was Dorothy the one to tell you about the stranger at our house?" she asked while we waited for the computer to warm up.

A reporter should never reveal their sources, but I nodded nevertheless. Why start trouble with someone who is trying to help?

"Why do you ask, Penny?"

"The cops were over there and I asked one of them about it. They were kind enough to tell me that she thought she saw someone breaking in that day."

We both stared at the computer screen, waiting for it to come to life.

"Personally, I wouldn't believe a word that comes out of that woman's mouth," Penny said. "She's so full of it."

"Full of what?"

"Her whole I-can't-leave-the-house-thing."

"Why do you say that?" I asked, truly confused.

Dorothy seemed completely terrorized by the thought of venturing beyond her front door.

"Watch this," Penny said. "This is at five in the morning the day my mother died."

The recording showed the quiet, dark street outside. A racoon ran across the Tillwacker porch, which started the recording. Penny's porch was lit, as was Dorothy's. A car drove past, but there wasn't any other movement... until Dorothy walked out her front door dressed in a big parka and headed down the street toward Myra's.

"Oh, wow," I murmured as she strode off the screen and it went dark.

"She tells everyone she's afraid to leave her house, but she's out almost every morning before the neighborhood wakes," Penny said. "I used to feel sorry for her until we got the doorbell and I saw her out for a stroll almost every morning. She's playing the sympathy card."

"She said she and your mom were close," I murmured as Penny scrolled through the footage. "That your mom brought her food and ran errands for her."

"Oh, yes, my mom felt really sorry for that woman and did a lot of things for her. Then, we got the doorbell and she realized Dorothy was taking advantage of her kindness. She had a few choice words for her. There was an argument and my mom threatened to let everyone know what a manipulator Dorothy was."

"What did Dorothy say to that?"

"That my mom would regret it if she ever did."

What exactly did that mean? Could it translate to murder? If Dorothy was taking advantage of people's kindness, she wouldn't want that getting out. She'd become the town pariah.

"Here we go," Penny said. This is where Mrs. Marple was leaving."

The doorbell activated as Mrs. Marple grabbed the handrail and carefully walked down the steps. Penny fast-forwarded a little bit to where a man approached the house wearing a black baseball hat and parka, his head down. He knocked on the door and turned his head to the side.

Something seemed oddly familiar about him.

"Show me your face," I murmured, moving in closer to the screen. "Who are you?"

"I don't know him," Penny said. "One of the cops seemed to, though, when we showed this to him."

The guy rubbed his hands together and knocked on the door again.

"Why isn't your mom answering?" I asked.

"The cops said she either didn't answer for strangers, or she had already been killed."

"How long after Mrs. Marple left did this happen?"

"About forty minutes."

He knocked one last time, then glanced up as he looked through the side window. I gasped and stepped back, almost knocking over a chair when his face came into full view.

"What's wrong?" Penny asked, pausing the recording.

"I... I know him," I whispered.

15

———

Derek?!

What the heck was Derek doing at the Tillwacker house the day of the murder?

"Who is it?" Penny asked, pushing play again.

Derek slipped a clipboard from inside his jacket, the metal clip shining in the sun. Had that been the metal thing Dorothy thought she'd seen?

He pulled something from the clipboard and shoved it into the door. "Sir, please leave my porch," Ted's voice said over the speaker. "We don't appreciate solicitors." Derek then startled and almost jumped away from the door.

My boyfriend stared at the doorbell for a second, then nodded. "Okay, sure!"

He trotted down the stairs—without falling, I noted—and out of range. The screen went black.

"Who is that?" Penny asked again.

"His name's Derek," I said. "He's my boyfriend."

"It looked like he was dropping something off. My dad hates unsolicited stuff."

Did Derek even realize he had been at the Tillwacker house the day Lydia had been murdered?

And I now understood why Byron had gazed at Derek the prior night when discussing the suspects. We've got some great leads and we'll be making an arrest soon. He'd seen Derek on the recording and I knew without a doubt that if Byron could pin Lydia's murder on him, he wouldn't have second thoughts.

"This is about fifteen minutes later," Penny said as I appeared on screen when my truck pulled up in front of the house. She grimaced as I fell backward down the stairs. "That had to hurt."

"I still have the bruises," I said, sighing.

We watched as I knocked, and then finally tried the door.

"What made you come in?" Penny asked as tears welled in her eyes, then the screen went dark.

"I was actually a little worried and I'll admit, a bit annoyed," I said, giving her forearm a quick squeeze. "Your mom and I had an appointment, and I thought maybe she had gotten sick or hurt herself when she didn't answer."

Penny nodded. "As you can see, whoever did it, they didn't come through the front door. They came in through the back. The next recording is when the police arrived."

"Was the lock on the back door jimmied, or did your mom have it open?"

"There wasn't a scratch on it, so the sheriff says my mom either knew the person and opened the door to them, or it wasn't locked."

I stared at the blank computer screen and tried to piece it all together. "Can you go back to when I arrived?"

"Sure."

We watched as I exited my truck again. "Stop it right there, please."

I stared at the picture. The camera was angled directly out front and didn't show any part of the adjacent houses. If someone knew about the doorbell, it could be avoided by sticking to the side yard and entering through the gate.

Which also meant that Byron and the sheriff could pin this on Derek. They could insinuate that after Derek had been dismissed by Ted, he crept to the side of the house and snuck in the back door.

Thankfully, there wasn't a motive to be found... well, at least I couldn't fathom one.

"Thanks for your help, Penny," I said. "I really appreciate it."

"If you need anything else, just stop by," she said. "I get the creeps staying here by myself, so I'm always glad for the company."

Biting my tongue, I refrained from giving her another lecture on moving out and finding her own way. She'd already heard it and I wasn't a parental figure.

As I pulled away from her house, I realized I needed to clear my head. Too many thoughts swirled, too many what if's and stabs at whodunit. I decided to drive out of town a bit and attempt to make sense of the web in which I found myself entangled.

The long stretch of highway sandwiched between forest lay before me, giving me the tunnel vision I needed to sort things in my mind. I had two new suspects to add to my list. First off, Dorothy. It really burned that she lied to me, Debbie, and everyone else about her fears of leaving the house, and I understood why Lydia felt she had been used. I imagined the old Lydia would have let the lie slide, but the new, more assertive Lydia had confronted Dorothy. Honestly, the woman had a lot to lose if people discovered she'd been playing them... but still, was it enough to kill Lydia? Dorothy had certainly acted as if she had no clue about the doorbell, but had it only been more deception? If she knew, would she actually be bold enough to take her early morning walks? I certainly wouldn't, but I didn't carry such a heavy lie on my shoulders.

And now Derek had been thrown into the mix. I didn't think he had committed murder. In the past, he'd donated a lot of his time to different causes such as going door to door to get residents signed up to vote, collect contributions for the food bank in Cedarville, or ask people if they had any old blankets to donate for the homeless shelter. However, his arrival within the timeframe the murder had been committed made it easy for the sheriff to look at him.

But then, Mr. Tillwacker had motive. What if he'd actually been home, instead of at work, as he'd claimed? What if he had been inside the house killing his wife while Derek had knocked on the door? Perhaps his car had been parked in the garage, or even around the corner from his house? Had he waited until Mrs. Marple had departed, then killed his new, assertive wife—a woman so different from the one he'd married?

Hank's words rang in my head. Mrs. Tillwacker went from a person who allowed everyone to walk all over her to an assertive woman who wanted to take control of her life. I promise you, her husband didn't like that one bit.

Had the sheriff's office even investigated where Ted had been during the time of the murder?

Mrs. Marple had fully admitted to fighting with Lydia about the direction the knitting club had gone. Had she been angry enough to kill her? Or what about Nancy Jones? She'd had her sights set on world domination in the knitting club world and Lydia had stood in her way. Again, it seemed silly to murder someone over such things, but every day the news was filled with people who'd been killed for much less.

Then there was the clerk Lydia had gotten fired and he'd made threats to her. However, would he know about the doorbell? Doubtful.

Which brought me back to my main suspect: Ted Tillwacker. He had motive and opportunity. How did I prove he did it? Or should I simply sit back and wait for the sheriff to make an arrest and accept my defeat?

Probably not the best idea now that Derek could be placed at the scene of the crime at the time it was committed.

With a sigh, I pulled over onto the side of the road and called my boyfriend.

"Hey, Tilly. What's up?"

"Did you know you were at the Tillwackers the day of the murder? Actually, right around when the murder was being committed?"

"Uh... no. Really? How did you discover that?"

"I looked at their doorbell recordings. You were there."

A long silence stretched between us and I glanced at my phone to be certain the connection remained, which was always touch and go on the highway toward Little River.

"I had no idea," Derek said, his voice soft. "I don't even know where she lived. I wonder if there's something I could have done to prevent the murder?"

Leave it to Derek to worry about others. He obviously hadn't concluded that the sheriff could be looking at him as a suspect. "I doubt it. But the sheriff knows you were there, Derek."

"Ah. I see. I wondered why Byron was giving me the side-eye when we talked about it last night."

"That's why," I said. "What were you doing?"

"Collecting blankets for the homeless shelter," he replied with a sigh. "Do you think I need to call my lawyer?"

"Not yet. Let's see if they arrest you first. How're things going at the old Rupert house?"

"Awful," Derek replied. "The pipes froze and burst. There's a good two feet of water in the house. Your dad says it's a goner."

"Oh, no."

"I don't know if it's worth putting money into it to try and save it, or just raze the place."

"You better get a couple of different bids," I replied.

"Agreed. What time do you think you'll be home tonight?"

"I'm not sure. I have a few things to do at the office, but it shouldn't be too late. I'll call you and let you know."

"Sounds good. Talk to you later."

I hung up and stared at the road. My drive hadn't given me any mind-blowing epiphanies, but instead skyrocketed my frustration.

"Dang it," I whispered, feeling lost, like a lone boat out at sea.

Who could I talk with that knew Ted Tillwacker well? No sense going to his daughter, Penny. She had told me she knew of no one who wanted to hurt her mother, except her father, but she'd also been terribly angry at the man when she'd made her declaration.

"Focus," I said. "You need to focus and think. The answer is out there."

I turned my car around and headed back to Oak Peak, determined to find the killer. Suddenly it came to me, and I knew exactly who I would go to for more information about Ted.

When I arrived at Oak Peak Avenue, I noted the street was very busy and there wasn't any parking in front of the paper. I drove past the Tri-Town Times and turned around a half-mile later, hoping a space had freed up.

Thankfully, a car pulled out a few doors away from the paper, and I grabbed the slot. When I exited my truck, I glanced up to find Byron walking down the sidewalk toward me. I narrowed my gaze on him as I decided what to do. Did I confront him about his horrible behavior, or cross the street and act like I didn't see him?

Six months ago, I would have bolted across the street to avoid the confrontation, but no longer. Lydia Tillwacker wasn't the only one who had been going through a metamorphosis.

Glaring at him, I stood in the middle of the sidewalk as he approached, staring at his phone. He was so engrossed, he almost ran into me.

"Tilly!" he exclaimed with a large grin. "It's so good to—˜

"Shut your trap, Byron Mills," I said through a clenched jaw. "If you think for a hot second that stunt you pulled last night is going to make a difference on how I feel about Derek, you've never been more wrong in your life."

"Someone needs to talk some sense into you, Tilly," he said, shoving his phone in his jacket pocket, his smile fading. "I thought maybe if your parents knew the truth, they'd do it."

"You thought wrong. I make decisions on who I date and who I don't—not them. And if you come sniffing around my place again like a dog in heat, I'll knock you upside your dumb head with my baseball bat. Are we clear?"

My hands shook with rage as I stepped around him and continued toward the paper.

"I'm going to make you see what a mistake you're making, Tilly!" he yelled. "I love you and I'll do everything in my power to make sure you don't marry that no good druggie!"

I flung open my office door, my anger seething

with such fury, I kicked the trashcan. Harold stared at me with wide eyes, obviously wondering where my pleasant demeanor had gone. "What's wrong, Tilly?"

"Nothing," I hissed, yanking my coat off. "I don't want to talk about it now."

After sitting down behind my desk, I stared at my computer screen, unable to concentrate on the email notifications through my fury. Love? Byron loved me? The idiot barely even knew me. I hadn't given him the chance because I had found him so boring.

I love you and I'll do everything in my power to make sure you don't marry that no good druggie.

What had he meant by that? Would he be charging Derek with murder, or was it something far more sinister?

To what depths would Byron go?

16

____

THE NEXT MORNING, I strode across my yard and into where the old Rupert orchard used to be, hand-in-hand with Derek. Tinker ran circles around us, glad to be out with her humans.

Admittedly, it was nice for us to have some time alone. With my parents in town, we hadn't had but a few minutes here and there.

"Are you feeling better today?" he asked.

I nodded, my cheeks numbed in the early morning cold. "Yes. I was really angry yesterday."

"Do you want to tell me why?"

Yes, but no. I'd decided Byron wouldn't take up any more room in my head and that meant his name wouldn't cross my lips. Christmas, the happiest time of year for me, was coming full steam and I had a murder to solve. "Maybe some other time," I replied. "It's really not important. I just let something get to me that I shouldn't have."

Derek squeezed my hand. "Okay, you let me know if you want to talk about it."

We walked the rest of the property in silence while I appreciated him giving me my much-needed space. I hadn't been successful in hiding my anger the previous night, no matter how hard I smiled and laughed. He'd seen right through me, but he'd instinctively known to keep his distance. Derek knew me so well.

Minnie's cows mooed at us from the other side of the fence, then strolled over to the barrier to greet us.

"Let's pretend we didn't see them," Derek said under his breath. "They always sneeze on me and it's gross."

"That's a good idea. They do the same to me. I hate those dumb cows."

"Are you ready for this?" he asked when we reached the back door. "I can't believe the damage."

"Ugh. Let's see it."

As he slid open the door, a wall of shockingly cold air blasted us. The water had been pumped out of the home, but the floor squished beneath my boots. Derek hadn't been joking when he'd said there had been a couple feet of water in the house—the waterline was evident on the walls.

"What a mess," I murmured. "All the furniture has to be hauled to the dump."

"I agree. Your dad said he'd never seen flooding this bad except in a hurricane. It's like someone turned on the tap to all the faucets and walked out."

Narrowing my gaze, I glanced around the ruined home, Byron's words still playing in my mind.

I love you and I'll do everything in my power to make sure you don't marry that no good druggie.

Did that mean ruining property Derek owned? But how would that prevent me from being with him?

It wouldn't. Apparently, I was looking to blame Byron for everything under the sun, including busted pipes.

"And you saw the pipes?" I asked casually. "Are they really broken? Could some kids have come in here and turned on the faucets?"

"No, I'm sure. There isn't any forced entry on any of the doors, all the windows are intact, and your dad showed me where the pipes cracked."

"This is such a shame, Derek," I said, shaking my

head as I shoved my hands into my parka pockets. "Do you know what you're going to do yet?"

"Nope. I was hoping you'd help me decide. I have two guys coming out today to give me bids on fixing it up and tearing it down. Of course, the insurance will help out, but whatever road we choose, it's going to be expensive."

Dang it. I hated wasting money and it seemed no matter what he decided to do on the house, he would be doing just that. Could the house be livable once again without dumping a small fortune into it?

"I should have come over here more often," Derek said, glancing around. "This could have been avoided if I had."

"You couldn't have foreseen this mess," I murmured. "Quit blaming yourself."

"I'm not, but it's an expensive lesson."

We walked down the hall to the back bedrooms. They had received some water damage, but nothing like the living room and kitchen.

"I better get to work," I said, once we'd completed our tour of the destruction. "Let's sit down and look at everything tonight, okay?"

"Yes, ma'am."

We closed up the house and walked back through the old orchard. After slipping through the fence on my land, we once again ignored Minnie's cows calling to us. We both went inside and I said goodbye to my parents, then left for the day.

First stop once I got into town: Myra Kent's house. I'd seen her come and go from the Tillwackers' quite a few times so I assumed she knew Ted very well, and I had some questions.

I knocked on her door and smiled when she answered, obviously surprised to see me.

"Tilly!" she exclaimed, bringing her hand to her chest. "What a surprise!"

"Sorry to barge in like this, but I was wondering if you and I could talk for a bit."

She glanced over her shoulder then shrugged. "I guess so. The house is a mess, but come on in."

"A little mess never bothered me," I said with a grin as I followed her to the kitchen. An ironing board had been set up in the corner and a stack of shirts hung over the chair. "Ironing's the worst."

"Yes, but it needs to be done," she said, moving the clothing to the counter, then motioning me to follow her into the living room. "What can I do for you?"

"Well, I wanted to talk about Ted Tillwacker," I ventured as I slipped off my parka and sat down on the sofa.

"What about him?" she asked, her brow furrowed.

"When I came to see you right after Lydia's death, Joanne was here. She said that there were rumors he was having an affair, and I was wondering what you thought about it. I know you don't like to gossip and I appreciate that, but—"

"Ted Tillwacker is a member of my church," Myra said, her cheeks reddened. "He's an upstanding man of our community who is devoted to his faith. I know nothing of him having an affair, which would go against everything pure and moral."

"I see," I said, deciding to venture a little further. "It's just that a lot of times gossip does hold a hint of truth."

"Gossip drips from the tongue of Satan," Myra bit out.

I wondered what Debbie would think about that statement. She lived and breathed rumors, but was also one of the nicest, most caring people I knew. Of course, I was there right beside her along for the ride, so what did that make me, according to Myra?

"Do you think he could have killed Lydia?" I asked innocently. "From what I understand, he wasn't happy in his marriage."

"Lydia changed a lot this past year as I told you

the first time we met. She used to be sweet, caring, and a good wife, keeping her devotion to her faith and her husband first and foremost. Something happened to facilitate that change, causing her to lash out when she should hold her tongue, to back-talk her husband, which no man should accept. Perhaps it was the hormones that go wonky during a woman's change of life.

"However, as I have already said, Ted is a man of faith, an upstanding citizen. He may not have liked the metamorphosis Lydia was going through, but he'd never kill her. His faith wouldn't allow for it."

Myra seemed very certain Ted was innocent. I still had doubts but decided to move the conversation to another topic.

"Do you know Dorothy down the street?" I asked. "She lives right across from the Tillwackers."

"Of course," Myra replied, her shoulders sagging slightly, as if relieved our discussion had moved on. "She used to be a member of the knitting club before her husband died, God rest his soul. Then she came down with that horrible agoraphobia and couldn't leave her house, so she couldn't join the knitting meetings any longer."

Apparently, Myra was far more comfortable

discussing Dorothy and her issues than Ted and his possible infidelities and murder.

"Did you ever consider having the meetings at her house?"

"I... I don't think so. It was almost a year ago, but I can't remember it ever being discussed. I just recall her phoning me and saying that she wouldn't be joining us any longer and explaining why. It's too bad she can't get help for the condition."

"Yes," I murmured, glancing around. I noted pictures of what I assumed to be her adult children on the mantle, but I didn't see any of a husband. I recalled Debbie telling me Myra's husband had left her, but I didn't feel comfortable asking for details. "Do you think Dorothy could have killed Lydia?"

Myra's face paled as her eyes widened. "Oh, my word. No. Absolutely not. She can't leave her house. Why would she do that? Why would you ask?"

"Just looking at all the possibilities," I replied with a shrug. "She had an argument with Lydia a few days before she was murdered."

I studied Myra closely. She had the hue of someone about to vomit.

"No, I don't believe it's possible," she said. "Not at all."

"Just between you and me, who do you think it

was?" I asked as I leaned forward and placed my elbows on my knees.

"Well, I don't know. Ted told me there was a man in Little River who'd threatened Lydia, and there was also a man who'd come to their house about the time Lydia was killed. He chased him away with the doorbell contraption they have."

"Yes, I heard about that." She didn't need to know it had been Derek.

"He could have easily snuck around the side of the house and gone in the back door," she continued. "That's what Ted is thinking, and I have no reason to question him."

Myra seemed to take everything Ted said as gospel, which made sense if they attended the same church and that was one of the tenets held in the religion.

"You seem to be asking a lot of questions that the police would," Myra added, a little smile turning her lips. "Are you trying to solve this murder, Tilly?"

She'd leaned forward as if we were two women about to share a secret. Except, I was going to keep the information to myself. "Have the police been here and asked you about any of it?"

Myra shook her head and sat back as if I offended her by not answering her question. "No.

They haven't talked to me at all, which is fine. I have nothing to add to their investigation, except my prayers."

"Of course," I said, standing and grabbing my bag and parka. "I really appreciate your time, Myra."

"You're welcome. I'm not sure how much help I am, but I do know in my soul that Ted didn't kill Lydia. No man of faith would stoop to such diabolic levels. He'd have to be possessed by Satan himself to murder his wife."

Satan sure ruled a lot of different things in Myra's world: gossip, and now, killers. He seemed to be the catch-all for everything.

I waved over my shoulder as I walked down the pathway to my truck. Myra hadn't shared anything new with me, but something still didn't sit right. What was it?

As I drove back to the office, I replayed our conversation. Nothing stood out to me as strange, but I couldn't shake the feeling that something was off.

I'd file it away for later examination because I had a killer to catch.

17

———

AFTER STOPPING by the office to see if Harold needed me for anything, I headed over to Debbie's Deliciousness. Hank sat in the middle of a group of women—I counted ten—who were all caught in the midst of a fit of giggles.

Hank waved as I walked over to the counter where Debbie and Carla stood, also both smiling.

"What's going on?" I asked.

"Your stepdad and Derek stopped in for a coffee on the way to the hardware store," Debbie replied. "The portion of the knitting club who has gone AWOL came in right after, and now Hank has them in stitches with stories from Louisiana. No one can believe he's got a pet alligator."

"I never would have if I didn't hear it from Tilly," Carla said.

Debbie nodded. "You're right. I wouldn't either. The women are loving him, though."

"Where's Derek?" I asked.

"He waited for a few minutes, but then realized Hank was here for the long haul," Debbie said. "He went to the hardware store and said he'd be back later."

I glanced over at the group again, noting Mrs. Marple sat front and center, her gaze dancing with laughter as Hank spoke, and I turned back to Debbie. "What do you know about Myra Kent?"

"Not much," she said with a shrug. "I know she's really active in the church. Her husband left her a while back. Maybe three years? Four?"

"Do you know why?"

"No."

"She says that gossip falls from Satan's lips," I said. "That's what she told me, anyway."

"Well, let me tuck in my forked tongue," Debbie muttered, rolling her eyes.

"Do you go to church, Tilly?" Carla asked.

I shook my head. "No. I believe, but I don't go to church."

"That's what I thought," she said. "Mac and I

belong to a non-denominational one if you ever want to join us."

"Thanks, I'll keep it in mind."

When I was young and living in Kansas, my dad had insisted on us attending church. I don't recall much but the sermons that seemed to go on forever. After my dad passed away and my mom moved us to Louisiana, we never attended again. My mama and I had talks about spirituality and believing in a higher deity, but we never practiced any formal religion.

Hank continued telling his stories to the mesmerized group. "And then, Irwin got onto the boat, and that poor man was so terrified, I thought he was going to jump over the side. But Irwin just wanted some marshmallows. I told that man he could smell fear, so he better buckle up and get his act together."

"What happened then?" one of the ladies asked.

"That man passed out," Hank said, throwing his hands up in the air. "Right there on floor of my boat. I thought I had a dead tourist, but it was just one scared into unconsciousness."

Laughter wafted through the bakery once more.

"If you want information on Myra, the best person to ask is probably Mrs. Marple," Debbie said. "They've known each other forever and a day."

"I think they used to go to the same church," Carla chimed in. "Mrs. Marple goes to mine now, but I think I remember her saying she used pray at Holy Trinity."

"Why are you so interested in her?" Debbie asked.

"I honestly don't know," I replied. "I visited with her today and I... something just seems off."

"You think she killed Lydia?" Carla asked.

"No," I replied with a sigh. "I think Ted Tillwacker did it. But something is just... I can't even put it into words."

We waited until Hank had finished his story of the haunted swamp. "And if you go out there at night, which I don't recommend," he said, his voice dropping to almost a whisper, "you can see her rising from the water, her black hair flowing around her shoulders as she moves deeper into the swamp where she was killed."

"Oh, my goodness," one of the women said. "I'm going to have nightmares."

"Mrs. Marple," Debbie called. "Can we speak to you for a minute?"

The woman hurried over while rubbing her arms. "That one gave me goosebumps," she said.

"You grew up with quite a character there, Tilly. He's an absolute hoot! I envy your childhood."

I glanced over at Hank, who gave me a quick wink, then returned his attention to his audience. "Never a dull moment," I replied with a smile. "Always lots of stories and laughter. He's a great guy."

"He most certainly is," Mrs. Marple said. "Now, what do you girls need? I don't want to miss the next tale."

"We were wondering if you recalled what happened to Myra Kent's husband," Debbie said. "He left her a few years ago, right?"

"He did," Mrs. Marple replied. "From what I understand, he's living on the beaches of Mexico with a woman younger than his daughter selling margaritas to make ends meet. It had been the scandal of the year when he took off, but his son came for a visit not too long ago and I ran into him at the grocery store. I inquired about his father and the boy said the man is very happy—happiest he's ever seen him."

I didn't bother mentioning that "the boy" in question was in his thirties, but I supposed once one reached Mrs. Marple's age, everyone seemed young.

"Why did he leave?" Carla asked.

"Well, seems he couldn't take any more of the draconian life they'd set up for themselves—his words, not mine. He didn't want to be someone's employee for the rest of his life and didn't like the strict schedule and rules. He wanted to live on his own terms and have tequila for breakfast, or some nonsense like that."

"So why didn't he ask Myra to go with him?" Carla asked.

"Oh, he did. He said he loved her and wanted her to join him."

"And Myra obviously said no," Carla mused. "If Mac asked me to go live on a beach in Mexico, I'd be packed before him."

"Well, it wasn't the right decision for Myra," Mrs. Marple said. "She likes her life orderly and stable. She decided that any man who would give up everything they'd worked for just like that didn't belong in her life. She said he'd been possessed by Satan himself and she didn't want him around."

"Interesting," I murmured. Everything seemed to come back to Satan.

Mrs. Marple glanced at all of us. "Why do you girls ask?"

"I was at her house today and there's just something off there," I said. "I can't even explain it."

"Well, she never remarried and she devotes a lot of time to her church. She enjoyed the knitting club, except when we gossiped. She didn't like that one bit, and sometimes, if we didn't stop, she'd simply get up and leave without a word. She's nice enough, but an odd bird."

"What's going on here, Tilly?" Hank asked, strolling over to the counter. "You're ruining my storytelling flow."

"Sorry about that," I replied. "I just had some questions about one of the Tillwackers' neighbors."

"You know it was the mister who killed her," he said, tapping the counter with his forefinger. "Mark my words."

"What makes you think that?" Mrs. Marple asked.

Hank ran his hand over his beard as he spoke. "I've heard her described as a doormat, until something happened and she came to life and was tired of being taken advantage of, with people walking all over her. She stood up for herself and the husband didn't like that one bit. It has to be him."

"Well, I'm on the list of suspects the sheriff is cultivating, too," Mrs. Marple said with a smile and pride in her voice. "Can you believe it?"

"Sure I do," Hank replied, giving her a wink. "I

can tell you're one tough lady who gets things done and doesn't take nothing from no one."

"You're right about that," Mrs. Marple said, tilting her chin upward. "My ancestors founded this town and I think that affords me a lot of respect."

"Yes, ma'am, it most certainly does," Hank agreed. "May I escort you back to the group and I'll regale you with some more Louisiana lore?"

"I'd love that," Mrs. Marple said, snaking her arm through his, then she glanced over her shoulder at Debbie. "Could you bring me another coffee, dear?"

"Will do," Debbie said with a chuckle, then she turned to me. "Man, your stepdad is quite the charmer."

"I know. He's in his element telling stories to anyone who will listen. That's why he does so well as a swamp tour guide. He never gets tired of sharing the same tales over and over, and sometimes even makes up his own."

"He's awesome," Carla said.

"Have you two seen my mom today?" I asked.

Both shook their heads. "The way I understood it, she stayed at home while the boys took a quick trip to the hardware store, then your stepdad got sidetracked with the ladies," Debbie said as she poured Mrs. Marple a coffee, then hurried over to serve it.

"Now, the one thing you have to watch out for when ya'll come down and visit the swamps of Louisiana is Julia Brown," Hank said. "I've been through every swamp in the great state, and Julia scared the daylights out of me. Some refer to her as Julia Black, or Julia White. But anyhow, she was a voodoo priestess, and you don't want to mess with one of them. They'll get you tied up in spiritual knots like you can't believe.

"Julia used her powers for good—most of the time. She helped people with their medical issues and delivered some babies. When she wasn't working, she sat on her porch and sang songs. Legend has it, she used to sing one, and the lyrics went something like this: 'one day I'm going to die and take the whole town with me.'"

"Oh, my!" one of the ladies exclaimed.

"Yes," Hank said, lowering his voice. "And she did just that. The day she passed in 1915, a horrible hurricane struck. It killed just over three hundred people and wiped towns right off the map. Completely decimated them until there wasn't anything left but rubble. The storm has been attributed to her passing. She took her town and then some. If you're quiet while in the swamp where she once lived, you can sometimes hear her singing. She might even rock the boat a little."

"Have you ever heard her?" Mrs. Marple asked.

"Oh, yes," Hank said with a nod. "Pretty voice with an echo, like she's calling from the other side, bless her soul. It sends shivers down my spine just recalling it." He held up his arm and rolled up his sleeve. "Even gives me goosebumps!"

"How terrifying!" Mrs. Marple exclaimed.

"You have that right, lady," Hank replied with a nod. "But what's even scarier, is she'll push on the boat while she sings. You don't know if you're going to end up in the water that's flooded with other spirits and hungry monsters, or if she's going to spare you. Sometimes, you can even feel her breath on your face while she's deciding whether or not to send you to a watery grave."

"Louisiana is filled with so many ghosts and critters," another woman said.

"That's true," Hank replied. "Lots of history there. I hope one day you'll come down and let me give you a proper tour of the swamps. They can be scary, but they're also beautiful with the cypress trees dripping with Spanish moss."

"I was there once," another woman said. "I didn't

think those trees were pretty at all. The whole place was frightening."

Hank let out a loud guffaw, then took a sip of his coffee. "Let's agree to disagree. It's all frighteningly beautiful. Sound good?"

"Definitely!"

"Tell us some other stories," Mrs. Marple urged. "And just for the record, I've now put a visit to Louisiana on my bucket list."

"Well, if you come, you'll have to take a cemetery tour," Hank said. "To some, it's the strangest thing about us."

"Why is that?"

"We bury our dead above ground."

A few women gasped and Hank dove into another story of ghosts murdering visitors and taking them into their own graves in the deep of the night.

"I'll see you two later," I said, waving at Carla and Debbie. "Don't listen too hard or you'll have nightmares."

"I think I'm kind of expecting them," Carla said, biting her lip. "These stories are creepy as heck. I just wish I knew whether they were real or not."

"Only Hank knows."

I left the bakery and went back to work, glad my

stepdad could keep the AWOL knitting club members so enthralled.

However, now that they were listening to him, they weren't talking among themselves, which meant I could be missing out on some vital gossip.

With a giggle, I imagined all the women speaking to each other with forked tongues.

Voodoo priestesses and zombies. Just another day in Hank's life.

Yet, none of those stories were going to help me solve the murder.

18

—————

I WAITED in the reception of Doctor Wheeler's office with two other people. His receptionist announced twice he was running late and apologized profusely. With the explanation I didn't mind the delay one bit, especially recalling my time waiting in the mayor's office and how his snooty wife had kept ignoring me. I could be patient, especially if treated with respect.

After twiddling my thumbs for forty-five minutes, Doctor Wheeler, or Ironman, as I secretly called him, hurried out while running his fingers through his salt and pepper hair. "Tilly, I'm so sorry," he said. "We had a couple of walk-in flu cases I had to look at during our meeting time. I can see you now."

As I stood, I stretched out my hand and he shook

it. "That's okay. I appreciate you letting me steal a few minutes."

"Come back with me. I hope you don't mind me eating while we talk. My afternoon is booked up."

"Not at all."

I followed him through the reception area and down the hall to his office all the while trying to hold my breath. The last thing I needed was to inhale the flu virus and find myself sick for Christmas.

His neat and tidy office was small but comfortable. I sat down and pulled out my notebook while he maneuvered to the other side of the desk and retrieved a sandwich from a cooler sitting on the back credenza, then took his chair. "Harold said you had some questions on the Lydia Tillwacker autopsy?"

"Well, I don't have anything specific, but I was wondering if you could tell me about the findings."

Doc Wagner studied me a brief moment before speaking. He unwrapped his sandwich. "It's an ongoing police investigation, Tilly. All information you get should come directly from the sheriff."

"Yes, I know. However, as you're aware, my relationship with them isn't the best."

A small smile crept over his lips as he chewed.

"And, I'm not printing anything you tell me," I continued. "It's for reference for when the sheriff's office solves the case and I write about it."

"I see," he said, patting his mouth with a napkin. "Well, as long as you aren't printing anything I tell you before the sheriff's office brings the case to a close, I don't see any harm in speaking to you in general terms while keeping the patient healthcare records sealed."

"Thank you," I replied, relief washing through me. "I'm not interested in any medical issues she may or may not have had. I'm curious about how she was killed, and I'm fine speaking in very general terms."

"Very well," he said with a nod. "Lydia Tillwacker died from a blow to the head. Her DNA and hair were found on the fireplace poker. So, unless she was scratching her head with the darn thing, I have to go with that being the murder weapon. All the other tools in the set had her fingerprints, but no hair."

I wrote down his findings.

"Were there any other fingerprints on the murder weapon?" I asked.

"Yes. Ted and Penny's were both prominent, but no one else."

"So the murderer wore gloves?"

"That's the theory. Unless Ted or Penny did it."

"What do you think?" I asked, holding my breath once again. Did the doctor see the evidence led to Ted as I did?

"I don't know," he replied. "It's really not my place to solve the crime. I provide information, and that's it."

"Well, there aren't any other fingerprints on the poker and the doorbell didn't record anyone outside the home."

"I thought it did," Doctor Wheeler said, furrowing his brow. "The sheriff said a man came by and he wanted to investigate him."

"That was my boyfriend, Derek York," I said, rolling my eyes. "He was trying to collect blankets for the homeless shelter. He didn't even know he was at the Tillwacker house until I told him. He didn't kill anyone."

"Ah. Probably not him, then."

"No. Ted Tillwacker chased him away through the doorbell app by telling him to leave his property."

"I see."

"Since no one suspicious came to the front door, I think we can assume they knew about the doorbell and crept along the side yard to the back entrance. Either that, or Ted did it."

"Hmm... I don't know, Tilly. You seem pretty focused on him."

"Well, why shouldn't I be? There aren't any other fingerprints on the weapon, and I've met Penny. I don't think she could have killed her mom."

"Being the town doctor, I know that Penny has had mental health issues and has been capable of physical violence in the past."

I stared at the doctor as I tried to imagine sweet Penny becoming violent enough to kill her mother, and I simply couldn't. Maybe they'd argued, Penny had spiraled into a fit of rage and accidently murdered Lydia?

"Don't ask me anything further about the girl," Doctor Wheeler said. "I've spoken too much about her as it is and broken all sorts of rules and regulations. In fact, forget I even mentioned Penny."

"Of course," I murmured, surprised by the doctor's mistake. Perhaps he was trying to hint at a clue without telling me outright that he thought Penny killed her mother? "Do you know if she was even home? She wasn't there when I arrived, which was moments after the murder had taken place. I walked all through the house looking for Mrs. Tillwacker, but never saw her. She could have been there beforehand, though, and left prior to my arrival."

"You'll have to ask Penny about that."

Penny could have lied about being out and would be aware of the doorbell camera, making it easy to skirt it.

"Ted Tillwacker said he wasn't there, that he was at the office when it happened. He could have easily snuck in through the back," I continued.

"It's a possibility, but I can't say for sure."

Was I missing something? From what I'd discovered about Ted, he seemed like the only suspect.

"What aren't you telling me?" I asked. "Something makes you doubt it's him."

"Well, for starters, there is his alibi."

"He lives five minutes away from his office. He could easily have snuck back to his house without anyone knowing."

"Let me finish, Tilly," Doctor Wheeler said with a smile as he steepled his fingers. "That's not the only thing."

"Sorry. Please go on."

"The trajectory of the blow that killed her... I

don't think he delivered it. It's absolutely possible, but not very probable."

"Why not?"

"Ted Tillwacker is taller than Lydia, who stood about five-foot-five," Wheeler said. "The blow came from below or straight across and hit her right here," he turned and pointed about half-way down his head, "in the occipital region. The wound was horizontal."

I reached my hand up to my own head and felt the area. "Okay. I still don't get why he couldn't have done it."

"In my experience, the blow came from someone shorter or of equal height to her, not taller, which would have been the case if Ted Tillwacker had hit her."

"How do you figure?" I asked, still unable to picture exactly what he tried to convey.

"Stand up, Tilly," he said as he moved around his desk. I got to my feet while he grabbed a golf club from the corner by the door. "Turn around."

I faced away from him and my stomach twisted in knots. It wasn't I didn't trust the doctor but talking about murder and having him hold a golf club in his hand with my back to him... it became a little unnerving.

"If I were going to hit you from behind with this club, I would lift it over my head like this." I glanced back and saw the weapon raised above me. "That would result in the injury being in the parietal, or even the frontal lobe, which are in this area." He pointed to the top of his head and forward toward his eyes while lowering the club.

"Now, if I were of a smaller stature, let's say here," he continued as he crouched down a bit so he was just a couple inches taller than me, "hitting her over the head is certainly possible, but that's not where the injury was."

He shifted the club to his shoulder, as if he held a baseball bat. "Now, if I'm shorter and I swing like this, I'm going to hit the lower occipital region. If I'm taller and do the same, I'm going to most likely strike the parietal, unless I come from underneath like this."

As he slowly swung toward me, I finally understood his point. "Based on that line of thinking, you're assuming the killer is on the smaller side. Maybe her height or a little shorter?"

"Yes. And the fact that the death blow is horizontal instead of vertical is also telling. Someone hit her as though they were carrying a baseball bat, not wielding the weapon above his or her head as I just demonstrated." Wheeler set down the golf club where he'd found it. "Of course, I can't be one hundred percent certain, but that's my educated guess. We won't know until the sheriff finds the killer to see if I'm right."

We sat down at his desk again as I processed what he'd shown me. Unfortunately, his theory cut out Ted Tillwacker as the killer. It had to be someone of smaller stature who was present at the house, and that left me and Mrs. Marple as the two main suspects if the doctor was right. Penny was also just a couple inches taller than me, so she had to take a place on the list of potential murderers.

"I really appreciate your time today," I said, feeling a bit defeated. I thought I had Ted Tillwacker squarely in my sights as the guilty party, but that had been blown out of the water if Doctor Wheeler was correct.

"You sound disappointed, Tilly."

"Maybe a little bit," I replied with a shrug. "I thought it was Ted for sure."

"Keep in mind, I could be wrong, but I don't think so."

I doubted it as well, unless Ted hit her like he would a golf ball—with a deep swing downward, then up to her skull.

"It's not your place to find the murderer," Wheeler reminded me gently. "I know you've been successful in the past, but it's a really dangerous business."

"Yes, I know."

"Remember, you can't publish anything I've told you today," Doctor Wheeler said as he walked me out. "I just wanted to give you insight for when the murder is solved as a favor to your boss so you can write an informative, glowing article at that time."

"Got it. Thank you again."

As I walked over to my truck, I turned Lydia's case over in my mind.

Perhaps I wasn't cut out for solving murders. Maybe I'd been lucky the first two times. With Mr. York, I had to find the killer in order to save myself. With Jake Martinez, Carla had been in the sheriff's sights and I had to prove her innocence. I really didn't have any skin in this game. The sheriff had mentioned Derek, and they'd also questioned me, but it would be hard to pin the killing on either of us. Maybe it was time to let the police do their jobs instead of trying to rub my skills in their faces.

Yet, I couldn't let it settle.

There were two people around the house at the time of the murder who stood on the shorter end of the spectrum: Mrs. Marple and me. Penny had said she wasn't home and I had no reason to disbelieve her. She seemed truly broken up about her mother's death.

Since I didn't kill Lydia, that left Mrs. Marple. Yes, she'd been angry with Lydia about the knitting club, but she was also running around bragging and joking that the police thought she'd killed the woman. I had a hard time believing that she'd be acting that way if she'd actually done it. Or maybe she had and her shenanigans were her own way of deflecting investigation. She always let everyone know she deserved respect because it was her family who had actually founded Oak Peak. In her mind, did that give her the license to murder someone in a fit of anger?

This didn't sit right with me. Nothing about this killing did. It reminded me of a bunch of puzzle pieces scattered over a table and none of them would fit together, no matter how many times I tried.

"Start at the beginning," I said. "Think."

Doctor Wheeler was sure the person who had murdered Lydia had been on the smaller side.

So that left the question: who was short in stature, had a problem with Lydia, was an expert in deceit and intimately familiar with the Tillwackers' schedule?

"Dorothy Bennett," I said to the windshield. "It's the only answer that makes sense."

19

"GIRL, you're out of your dang mind," Debbie exclaimed the next evening. We sat in her bakery with my mom, Carla, and Mrs. Marple. "Dorothy didn't murder anyone!"

It was the first time I'd shared my thoughts, even keeping them from Derek. Guilt washed through me, but I'd tried to remain upbeat and positive while we dined with my parents the previous night and discussing murder could definitely be a downer. Derek had worked all day on the old Rupert house, moving furniture and salvaging what he could and I'd been so tired, we'd both crashed within seconds of lying down.

"Did you know she can go out of her house, that

she doesn't have agoraphobia?" I asked. "That she's been lying to you this whole time?"

Mrs. Marple gasped as her eyes widened, but Debbie waved her hand in front of her face as if to shoo away my question.

"Of course I knew that," Debbie snapped. "I thought everyone did and just played along."

"I most certainly didn't," Mrs. Marple said. "I had no idea. Why would she tell such tall tales?"

"Who knows?" Debbie replied. "But I figured if she was desperate enough to lie like that, then she had her reasons. I've seen her out walking when I drive into the bakery early in the morning. I just never mentioned it to anyone."

"Well, perhaps we should go ask her," Mama said. "Ask her why she's lied to the town and then if she murdered Lydia."

"I don't know about that idea," Mrs. Marple said. "What if she offs us?"

"There's five of us. She'd do no such thing," Carla said.

We sipped our coffee in silence for a few moments as we contemplated our next move. Having caffeine in the late evening would only mean a poor night's sleep for me, but I drank it anyway.

"Let's go for it," Debbie said. "I'm curious to see what she has to say."

"I can stay here and watch the bakery," Carla volunteered. "No reason I can't sell a few donuts while you all solve a murder... or at least confront a liar."

"Excellent," Debbie said. "We need this crime behind us so the town will know Lydia didn't choke on one of my donuts."

"That rumor is still going around?" I asked. "How many articles have I written debunking that?"

"There's a certain segment of people who don't trust the press," Debbie said. "They think you're full of nutmeg and nougat, filling them with thick lies because I'm your sweet friend."

"Really? I thought that only happened with the national media," I said, my feelings actually a little hurt especially since I'd always tried to be truthful, sincere, and neutral in my reporting. Sometimes I may have failed, especially when it came to writing about the sheriff, but Harold had always cleaned up my biases against him.

"It's okay, honey," Mama said, patting my hand from across the table. "We all know you have a good heart and you're honest to a fault."

"Exactly," Debbie agreed. "Don't worry about those who doubt you. There are plenty who don't."

"I say we go pay Dorothy a visit," Mrs. Marple said. "I'd like to hear her explanation of why she's been lying to everyone about her condition."

"Let's do it," Debbie said. "Just be nice to her, Mrs. Marple, unless of course she confesses to murder."

"If she does, I'll knock her over the head!" Mrs. Marple replied with a laugh. I stared at the older woman as she slipped on her coat. Even though everyone knew Lydia had died from a traumatic blow, it still unsettled me that it was the second time Mrs. Marple had mentioned knocking someone over the head, the first time being after her fight with Lydia about the knitting club.

Everyone seemed to think I was wrong about Dorothy being the killer. Maybe Mrs. Marple had done it and I was simply too close to see it.

We filed out of Debbie's Deliciousness and I rode over to Dorothy's with my mom.

"This is all so exciting," she said, rubbing her hands together before holding them in front of the heating vents. "We don't run around solving murders at home. I wish Hank were here. He'd love this."

"I honestly don't know who did it, Mama," I said with a sigh. "I don't like barging in on Dorothy like this, but after my visit with Doctor Wheeler and his explanation of the injury, I don't see who else it could be besides Mrs. Marple or me."

"Well, I know you're innocent, and I don't know Mrs. Marple well, but she seems harmless enough."

"I hope Dorothy doesn't feel threatened by us all showing up at her home like this," I said. "Personally, it would bother me."

"It depends on how everyone acts," Mama said. "If everyone is accusatory, she'll definitely feel vulnerable. But if we approach it with kindness and tenderness and a willingness to help her, perhaps she'll welcome the questions."

We pulled up in front of Dorothy's home, and Debbie parked just up the street. A long breath escaped me as I exited the truck, causing a white puff of condensation in the cold, night air, which reminded me of a ghost in one of Hank's tales as it evaporated.

Snow began to fall as Debbie led the charge up the front steps. Dorothy opened it before we had a chance to knock.

"My word!" she exclaimed. "What's going on?"

"We just came to talk to you for a bit," Debbie said. "How are you tonight?"

"I'm fine! This is such a nice surprise. Please! All of you, come in!"

After a quick introduction between my mom and Dorothy, we each found a place in the living room. "Would anyone like some hot tea?" Dorothy asked. "I'm happy to make some."

Everyone shook their head and our host settled in an overstuffed chair. "What can I do for you all?"

"Well, we wanted to talk to you about Lydia's death," I began. "There's just a few things we needed to discuss."

"What's that?"

I twisted my hands in my lap, unsure how to ask a woman if she'd committed murder. "Well, this is a delicate subject," I began. "First, I found out that you do not have agoraphobia. You're perfectly fine leaving your home."

Silence blanketed the room as Dorothy's smile faded and her cheeks flushed a deep red. Tears welled in her eyes, and she pinched her lips together.

"Why would you do that, Dorothy?" Mrs. Marple asked, her voice quiet. "Why would you lie about such a thing?"

As she began to sob, I stood and hurried into the kitchen in search of a box of tissues. I found one on the table and brought it in to her. Dorothy blew her nose as I sat down. Pity settled in my gut for her, but if she was a killer, she needed to be brought to justice.

"About a month after my husband died, the visits began to dry up, like they always do when someone loses a spouse," Dorothy said, her voice barely above a whisper. "When my friends stopped to talk, or bring me a casserole, it made my grief bearable. The kids had gone back to their own lives, and I was simply left... alone. I became incredibly depressed and found myself looking out the window most of the day."

"Why didn't you reach out to someone?" Debbie asked. "Why suffer like that?"

"Because I didn't want to be a bother to anyone," Dorothy said. "I didn't want to become that woman everyone came to dislike because she's so needy, and she can't get over the loneliness caused by her husband's death."

"We never would have thought that," Debbie said. "But I now understand why you made up the agoraphobia story."

"I thought people would be more likely to come

by if they knew I needed help," Dorothy said, wiping her eyes with a tissue. "Everyone was so kind when Burt died, and I hoped it would be the same if I came down with something that brought people to me, instead of me always having to pester others for company. I was right. Thank you so much for your visits, Debbie. I hate that I lied, but I appreciate you so much."

"I knew you were full of it about not being able to leave the house," Debbie said.

"How did you know?"

"I run a bakery," Debbie replied. "I have to be there before the sun rises. Sometimes I drive through your neighborhood to get there, and I've seen you walking."

"Ah," Dorothy said, blowing her nose. "I see. And here I thought I was being so smart about going out before daybreak."

"You never know who will be watching, especially today with fancy technology," Mrs. Marple said. "You were bound to be found out, dear. I wish you would have told me how lonely you were. I'd have been more than happy to go out to lunch or take in a movie with you."

Dorothy's tears started again. "I'm so sorry for my deception."

Mama and I exchanged glances, and she gave me a quick nod, as if to assure me now was the time to jump in with the big question.

"Having said all that," I began, "I've been told that Lydia knew you had lied to everyone in your life about this and that you threatened her when she said she would expose you. She found out by watching recordings taken by her doorbell of you walking the neighborhood in the early morning hours." The room fell silent as everyone stared at Dorothy. Her face flushed further and she shook her head. "So, we need to know... did you follow through with that threat?"

"You're asking if I killed Lydia because she promised to tell the town about my fake illness?"

"Yes, that's correct."

Wow, the living room had heated up quickly, as it often did during uncomfortable situations. I stood and moved to the window. Even double-paned glass couldn't keep out the cold of the night.

"I didn't murder Lydia," Dorothy said softly. "She was a good friend to me, but she had a lot of problems, especially lately."

"Like what?" Debbie asked.

"Penny, first of all," Dorothy said. "That poor girl has suffered mental issues since she was twelve.

She's finally able to hold down a job, but she's a bit of a wild child. She also continually argued with her mother. It wore Lydia down to the point of tears more than once."

"What other problems did she have?" I asked, wondering how much Dorothy truly knew.

"She'd had some type of… epiphany, I guess is a good word for it. She decided she didn't like her life and she had so many regrets. Instead of listening to her parents and marrying Ted, she wished she had gone into the workforce as she had originally wanted. She wasn't happy, she hated her life, and it began to show in almost every interaction she had."

"Like when she got the clerk at the store in Little River fired," Mrs. Marple said. "I heard that was a terrible interaction to watch."

"I heard the same," Dorothy said with a nod. "Then, of course, she threatened to let everyone in town know about my secret. She was rude and horrible to me that day, and I may have threatened her, but I never would have followed through with anything."

Dorothy stood and walked into the kitchen. On impulse, I followed, to gauge her height.

"Can I help you with anything?" I asked, gently holding her elbow. She was an inch or two taller than me, but no more. She fit the profile Doctor Wheeler had given.

"No, dear. I'm fine. I thought I would hate this day when it came, but it's actually cathartic. I'm sorry I lied, but I hope you can understand why."

"Of course," I replied. I really needed her confession. "Are you sure there isn't anything you want to tell me about Lydia to clear your conscience?"

She shook her head. "No, nothing. Lydia was a sad, angry woman. I'm sorry someone killed her, but it wasn't me."

With a smile, I tried to hide my frustration as I returned to the living room.

I still wasn't any closer to catching a killer and I didn't know where to turn to next. Who had killed Lydia Tillwacker?

20

———

THE WOMEN CONTINUED to talk in the living room as I stared out the window. The snow came down in thick, heavy sheets and if we didn't get moving soon, we'd have a heck of a time getting home.

Some of the houses on the block had been decorated with Santa in the yard, others with lights. I loved Christmastime and the bright emotions it brought to my soul, but this year it had been blanketed with Lydia's murder. I wanted to find that Christmas spirit I loved so much.

The lights in Myra's home went off, and a moment later, she walked down the sidewalk to the Tillwacker house dressed in boots and a thick parka carrying a large plastic laundry bag and a glass dish.

Ted answered the door and invited her in. Apparently, she was still feeding the man.

I sighed and leaned my head against the window again, imagining the Tillwacker house would be terribly depressing this time of year. Frankly, I was surprised the family even stayed there. If my spouse had been killed in our home, I'd want to move as soon as possible. Perhaps they didn't have the means to do so.

The women chattered on for a few minutes about Christmas plans, and it seemed Dorothy had been forgiven for her deception. I understood her lie, but I needed a way to prove she'd murdered Lydia. She was the only one left who fit the profile given to me by Doctor Warner. She had motive and opportunity. It wouldn't take her but a second to cross the street and go into the side fence. Perhaps she'd known about the doorbell and went walking anyway, hoping to get caught? She had said being confronted was a relief.

Just as I was about to announce we needed to leave, the lights in Myra's house turned on, yet, I hadn't seen her walk home. I knew she lived alone, but maybe she had family in town? But why turn off all the lights and leave someone in the dark?

How had she magically gone from the Tillwacker

house to her own? I'd been staring out the window and saw her walking down the sidewalk. I wouldn't have missed her.

I ran from the house to the end of the block and gasped at what I discovered. The backyard fences didn't butt up against each other as I had originally assumed. A small pathway weaved between them, which I followed.

Footsteps appeared in back of the Tillwacker house, and I tracked them all the way to Myra's back fence, my heart thundering.

Sitting down on a rock, I held my head in my hands as the snow fell around me and I recalled the day I'd found Lydia Tillwacker.

I'd always gone under the assumption that the killer knew about the doorbell and had snuck into the backyard through the side fence, avoiding the camera. However, now I knew of this pathway and things began to fall into place.

The sound of crunching boots came from my left, and I looked up to find my mom, Debbie, Mrs. Marple and Dorothy coming toward me.

"What's going on?" Mama asked. "What are you doing back here?"

"I didn't know this pathway existed behind the houses," I said, standing. "Whoever killed Lydia

Tillwacker took this path. I just remembered the snow in the side yard, where I thought the killer would have entered to avoid the doorbell, wasn't touched."

"So who did it?" Debbie asked.

I glanced down at the footprint leading to Myra's home, and stepped in it. The outline matched perfectly, and Myra was my height.

The only thing I didn't have was a motive. She'd been so upset the day I'd seen her after Lydia's murder.

"That's Myra's house, isn't it?" Mrs. Marple said.

"Yes, it is."

"Do you think she did it?"

"I don't know," I said with a shrug. "She fits the height requirement, but I can't figure out why she'd kill Lydia."

The gate opened and Myra stepped out, carrying a gun. We all back-pedaled with a collective gasp.

"What are all of you doing back here?" she asked.

"I didn't know there was a pathway behind the houses," I said. "That's how the murderer got into Lydia's home."

"How very interesting," Myra said as I gauged her height once again. With her athletic build, she wouldn't have any problem swinging a fireplace poker. "Lydia's death was God's work. No one else is responsible."

My mom and I exchanged glances.

"What does that mean?" Debbie asked.

"It means, Lydia had lost her way," Myra said. "Satan had taken her soul and she needed to be removed from this earth."

"And... did you help with that?" I asked. The religious undertones of this situation irritated me as I knew not everyone who practiced a religion felt the way Myra did. Instead, the word zealot came to mind.

Myra spun on my and held the gun out in front of her. "I went to her house that morning to try and talk some sense into her. She wanted to leave Ted and regretted ever marrying him. Ted didn't want the divorce, but she was insisting. How could she go against her husband's wishes like that? How could she defy him, therefore defying God? If she were a good wife, if she followed the tenets of the church, she'd be alive today."

"You killed Lydia?" Mrs. Marple said. "Because she didn't want to be married any longer?"

"I know how Ted felt," Myra said. "My husband also found Satan and left me. He now lives a life of sin and should be abolished before he can spread his evil."

"Someone better get in touch with him," Debbie muttered under her breath.

"What did you say?" Myra yelled. Her breath sawed in and out of her lungs causing puffs of white while the snow fell around us.

"Nothing! Nothing!" Debbie said holding her hands in the air. "Does your husband know how you feel about him?"

"Yes, and that's why he lives in another country."

"Smart man," Mama whispered.

"What about the day after?" I asked. "When I came to see you, you were in tears, heartbroken over your friend's death."

"Of course I was," Myra said. "My friend had fallen from her station as a loving mother and wife into the hands of Satan. If that's not something to cry about, I don't know what is.

"I went over there that morning and tried to pray with Lydia, but all she wanted to do was eat donuts and talk about how she was in charge of the knitting club. They'd all do as she said, or they'd be kicked out!

"On top of that, she wanted her daughter to see the world, and Lydia was going to take her, leaving

Ted to fend for himself. What type of wife does that? A woman's place is in the home, serving her husband!" We sat in stunned silence as Myra continued her tirade. "Ted is a man of God, a good man. He deserves the best of all things, and that includes a wife who treats him with respect! I'm now the woman doing that instead of his diabolical wife!"

Little things began to come back to me... like the mail I'd seen at Myra's house belonging to the Tillwackers. Had she grabbed it to pay Ted's bills? And the ironing I'd noticed in the kitchen... men's shirts. I hadn't paid much attention to it before, but now that I heard it from Myra, I realized she had indeed stepped into the Tillwacker caregiver role. She'd just delivered the man dinner and his laundry less than an hour ago!

"There aren't many people who are going to agree with you on that one," Debbie said. "Did you know he cheated on Lydia? That he was having an affair?"

I glanced at Debbie, uncertain if she was telling the truth or trying to bait Myra into something.

"That's nonsense," Myra hissed. "A man of faith would never do such a thing."

A large cracking sound startled all of us and a

small branch the size of a baseball bat from a neighbor's tree fell under the weight of the snow.

"We should head home now," I said. "It's cold."

"Do you really think I'm going to let you go anywhere?" Myra asked, once again turning her gun on me.

"What are you going to do, Myra?" Mrs. Marple asked. "Kill all of us?"

A brief flicker of doubt crossed her face, but then her resolve once again set in, along with the hint of crazy I hadn't noticed in my previous meetings with her. Without her saying a word, I realized killing all of us was exactly what she intended to do. Panic caused my heart to thunder and my stomach twisted with nerves.

"I have an idea," Debbie said. "Before you go putting a bunch of holes in us, let's go see Ted Tillwacker. He's a man of faith, as you said, Myra. He'll know what you should do."

"Excellent," Myra said. "You lead the way, you fork-tongued monster."

Debbie bit her lip and turned toward the Tillwacker house. Mama and I followed, even though I didn't like Myra behind me.

Dorothy hurried beside us. "What are we going to do?" she whispered. "The woman's a psycho! It's not very Christian-like to brandish a gun at others!"

"I don't know," I muttered.

We walked slowly through the thick snow. I had no idea what Debbie's grand plan was, but I hoped she let us in on it before we ended up with bullets in our backs.

A loud scream came from behind me and I turned to see Mrs. Marple swinging the tree branch at Myra's head. As the gun fell from her hand and she sank face-first into the snow, I yelled and jumped back, running into Debbie.

She pushed me aside and grabbed the gun, pointing it at Myra while Mrs. Marple stood over her, the tree branch raised above her head once again.

"Is she down?" Mrs. Marple yelled.

"Looks like it," Debbie responded, lowering the gun. "Nice hit, lady."

"Whew!" Mrs. Marple replied, dropping the branch. "Thank you!"

Myra began to moan and slowly rolled to her back. At least Mrs. Marple hadn't killed her.

"And you said this wasn't the wild west any longer," Mama murmured, wrapping her arm around my waist. "Boy, were you wrong!"

Relief swept through me that we were all safe while sirens wailed in the distance and became louder by the second.

"Who called the police?" I asked.

"Dorothy did before we all went out after you," Mama said. "You should have told us what you were up to, Tilly."

I nodded, realizing I'd acted very impulsively. "You're right. That was foolish."

The police cars stopped at the head of the pathway. Sheriff Connor and Byron came running at us through the snow.

"What's going on here?" the sheriff demanded as he eyed Myra and I avoided looking at Byron. "What have you women done?"

"We solved the murder," I said, pointing at Myra. "She admitted to all of us she killed Lydia."

"I did it for Ted!" Myra yelled. "I did it for him! He knew his wife was possessed by Satan! He wanted to be free of the evil that had penetrated his house! He wanted his daughter to have a normal, stable life... a traditional home!" She sat up and grabbed the back of her head. "I did it for Ted, for my faith in all that is good and righteous, for my God."

Sheriff Connor kneeled down next to her. "Are

you telling me Ted Tillwacker put you up to killing his wife?"

She nodded and began to sob. "I cannot be judged by anyone but God!"

"We'll see about that," Sheriff Connor muttered, then glanced up at Byron. "Go get him. Cuff him and bring him down to the station. I'll take care of Myra."

He helped the killer to her feet and placed the handcuffs on her while reading her rights, then led her through the snow to his police cruiser. A moment later, Byron came out of the Tillwackers' home with Ted in tow.

"We'll be in touch with you ladies tomorrow," the sheriff said. "We'll need your statements."

We all nodded and promised to be available when he called.

"You did it, my friend," Debbie said as she hugged me. "You solved another murder! You're the super sleuth of Oak Peak!"

"Let's all of us get home," Dorothy said. "I don't know about all of you, but I'm so cold, I feel like I'm a distant cousin to an ice cube."

"Would you mind if I came in for that cup of tea before I head home, Dorothy?" Mrs. Marple asked.

"I would love it," Dorothy said, linking arms with the older woman.

We all walked back to Dorothy's house and went our separate ways. Mama turned up the heat full blast in the truck, and we finally warmed up about half-way back to my place.

"What an adventure," Mama said, shaking her head. "The snow, the drama, that nonsense Myra spouted... I never imagined I'd be a part of something like that."

"Me neither," I replied with a sigh, absolutely exhausted.

"Hank's going to be thrilled he was right about Ted being the murderer."

He may not have given the death blow, but he'd manipulated a sick woman into doing his dirty work.

And for that, he'd get what was coming to him, both literally and figuratively. I couldn't imagine any god looking at his actions in a favorable light.

EPILOGUE

Christmas Day

Hank and Mama sat on the couch sipping hot chocolate while I flipped on Frank Sinatra and Dean Martin Christmas classics.

Derek had kept his promise and not given me any gifts, which I really did appreciate. However, I had one for him, and I hoped he'd accept it.

It was part of my plan to break all ties with Byron, to show him that not only could I solve a murder faster than him and his stupid sheriff, but his thoughts on my life meant absolutely nothing to me.

A turkey was roasting and the savory scent wafted through the house. Tinker sat in the middle of the kitchen hoping that it would miraculously shoot out of the oven and land in front of her.

"You keeping wishing that, you silly girl," I said, patting her head.

As I sliced the carrots, Derek came up behind me and gave me a kiss on the cheek. "How's my favorite chef today?"

"I'm good," I said. "Very, very happy. Thank you again for flying my parents out."

"Your happiness is the greatest gift you could give me. What can I do to help?"

"Well, let's get the potatoes mashed, then we're just waiting on the bird."

"I'm an excellent masher," Derek said and kissed my forehead. "I shall mash until there isn't a lump to be found."

I laughed and went back to my carrots. When we each finished our jobs, we returned to the living room to sit with my parents.

Belle had curled up in Hank's lap and slept soundly.

"You made a new friend," I said.

"I most certainly did. This cat is a tough nut to crack, but she finally fell for my charming ways."

"Everyone does, Hank," Mama said with a smile. "I know I certainly did."

Nervous butterflies tickled my belly as I tried to find the gumption to give Derek his present. I was finally, finally going to step past my fears.

With a big breath, I rose to my feet and set down my cup of hot cocoa, then I turned to Derek.

"What's up, Tilly?" he asked, his brow furrowed in confusion.

I took his mug from him, then pulled him to his feet, taking each of his hands in mine.

"Derek, two months ago you asked me to marry you," I said as my mom gasped. "At that time, we decided that it would be best to wait, that we had moved too fast."

"Well, you threw up on me, Tilly, then fainted out cold. What else was I supposed to think?"

"It wasn't one of my better moments," I said, grimacing. "And I'm sorry about that. But I was wondering if I could say yes today, if I could wear that ring you bought, and if we could plan our wedding?"

"Oh, my goodness!" Mama whispered.

Derek paled as his eyes widened, and fear gripped my chest. What if he said no?

"Seriously?" he asked. "Are you sure that's what you want?"

I nodded and became choked up as tears welled.

"Yes. Thank you for giving me time to find myself and being there every step of the way. Thank you for being my best friend."

Derek picked me up and swung me around, then set me down and stepped away from me, turning to my parents.

"Is this okay with you?" he asked. "Can I marry your daughter?"

Hank swiped at the tears rolling down his face while my mom screamed in delight, sending Belle out of the room with a hiss.

"Oh, son," Hank said, getting to his feet. "We'd love to welcome you to the family!"

My mom jumped up and hugged him, then me. "We've got a wedding to plan! Oh, my word. How exciting is this?"

"Well, I've thought a lot about this," I said. "And if it's okay with you, Derek, I would rather not get married in Oak Peak. I'd like to have the wedding in Louisiana at my parents' house. They've got a really pretty yard right on the water in Barataria—lots of trees and flowering plants. I've always thought it would make a beautiful backdrop for a wedding."

I'd been married once in Oak Peak, and it had ended in disaster. Repeating the process seemed like it would jinx any hope of a stable future for us.

"That's fine with me," Derek said, his smile stretching across his face. "This is the greatest Christmas present I've ever received. Thank you, Tilly. I'm going to work every day to be the best husband I can be."

"You're already pretty fantastic," I said. "Thank you for wanting to marry me."

We sat down and Mama talked about a caterer she knew while Hank said he'd cut back all the trees to make sure we had pictures with the water in the background.

It was going to be a perfect day, a perfect wedding.

Or so I thought.

Please continue Tilly's adventure in News and Noodles, found at all print retailers!